IMOGEN

The Story of Shakespeare's Cymbeline

J. Aldric Gaudet

Copyright ©2009 J. Aldric Gaudet

All rights reserved. No part of this work may be reproduced or transmitted in any form or by any means–graphic, electronic or mechanical, including photocopying, recording, taping or information storage and retrieval systems–without the prior written permission of the author.

ISBN 978-0-557-05866-2

INTRODUCTION

As said in the introduction to *Madmen Have No Ears: The Story of Shakespeare's Romeo and Juliet*, ever since school I've had a love/hate relationship with Shakespeare. Sadly, most of my schoolmates opted for the hate. I understand why, yet they missed out on some interesting stories, great characters and magnificent word play.

This is for them, and their children.

English has gone through 400 years of evolution since Shakespeare. Archaic words, unfamiliar phrases and antiquated references make comprehension difficult on first exposure and require serious study.

I began this project simply to clear up the thees and thous that cluttered the text in order to make the lines flow more smoothly for the 21st century ear, and have travelled a journey that took me to the Quartos and the Folios with all their variations; as well as numberless essays and dissertations by latter day scholars and editors; even to the consideration of the notorious work of Collier; all in order to try and understand the author's rooted meaning.

Whenever the experts disagreed, which was often, I used the meaning which best suited my understanding of the author's intent and reworked the line wherever necessary. The poetic imagery was favoured always, although verse and metre were sacrificed for clarity.

Nothing is footnoted. This is not meant as a reference work but as a reading adventure. In the spirit of the original, it celebrates the use of words and phrases to evoke unique images and explore dynamic characters confronting stressful situations.

My rationale rests on the shoulders of George Steevens who, in 1766, said of Shakespeare:
To make his meaning intelligible to his audience seems to have been his only care, and with the ease of conversation he has adopted its incorrectness.

It is all about choices. These are mine.

J. Aldric Gaudet - December 12, 2008

Britain. 16 A.D.

The garden of King Cymbeline's palace.

Two gentlemen are in conversation.

The First Gentleman says, "You do not meet a man who isn't frowning: faces no more obey nature than courtiers who reflect the king's mood."

The Second Gentleman says, "But what's the matter?"

The First Gentleman says, "His daughter, and heir to his kingdom–who he promised to his wife's only son, a widow he married late–has devoted herself to a poor but worthy gentleman: she's married; her husband banished; she imprisoned: all is pretend sorrow; though I think the king is touched deeply in the heart."

The Second Gentleman says, "Only the king?"

The First Gentleman says, "He that lost her too; so is the queen, who most wanted the match; but not one courtier, even though they all wear their faces to mirror the king's mood, has a heart that is not glad at the thing they scowl at."

The Second Gentleman says, "Why?"

The First Gentleman says, "The one that missed getting the princess is a thing too bad for bad report: and he that got her–I mean married her, and therefore banished–is a person that if you sought through the regions of the earth for one like him, there would be something failing in all that could compare. I do not think so handsome an outward appearance and such stuff within endows any other man."

2.

The Second Gentleman says, "You praise him far."

The First Gentleman says, "I do extend him, sir, within his own boundaries, and crush his virtues together rather than unfold all his measures duly."

The Second Gentleman says, "What's his name and background?"

The First Gentleman says, "I don't know his deeper roots: his father was Sicilius, who joined Cassibelan against the Romans. His titles came from Tenantius whom he served with such glory and admired success that he gained the surname Leonatus. He had, besides the gentleman we speak of, two other sons, who died in the wars with swords in hand. Their father, too fond of his children, took such sorrow that he quit being, and his gentle lady, carrying the gentleman of our discussion, died as he was born.

"The king takes the babe to his protection, calls him Posthumus Leonatus, brings him up and makes him part of his family, puts to him all the knowledge of his time; which he took, as we do air, as fast as it was administered, and in his young manhood began to harvest. He lived in court–which is rare–most praised, most loved, an example to the youngest, to the more mature a mirror that flattered them, and to the more serious a child that served his seniors. As for his mistress–for whom he is banished–her great cost proclaims how much she values him. As to his virtue; by her choice may be truly read what kind of man he is."

The Second Gentleman says, "I honour him just by your report. But is she the king's only child?"

The First Gentleman says, "He had two sons–if this is worth hearing, remember it–when the eldest was three, and the other in cradle-clothes, they were stolen from their nursery. To this moment no one knows which way they went."

The Second Gentleman says, "How long ago was this?"

The First Gentleman says, "Twenty years."

The Second Gentleman says, "That a king's children should be so stolen, so slackly guarded, and the search so slow, that could not trace them."

The First Gentleman says, "However it is strange, or that the negligence may be laughable, it is true, sir."

The Second Gentleman says, "I believe you."

The First Gentleman says, "We must go: here comes the gentleman, the queen, and princess."

Attendants come ahead of the Royals to clear the gardens. The two gentlemen go out the street gate.

*

The Queen, Princess Imogen and Posthumus enter. The Queen is dressed in elegant extravagance. Imogen, a charming beauty, is dressed more modestly yet still obviously a Princess. Posthumus, a fit young man, is dressed in plain clothes with plain accessories, practical rather than fashionable.

The Queen speaks to Imogen, "Be assured you won't find me, daughter, after the slander of most stepmothers, evil-eyed against you: you are my prisoner, but your jailer shall deliver the keys that restrain you."

She turns her attention to Posthumus, "For you, Posthumus, until I can win over the offended king, I will be known as your advocate: the fire of rage is in him still, and it is good you bowed to his order with what patience your wisdom guided you."

4.

Posthumus says, "Please your highness, I will leave today."
The Queen stops walking, "You know the risk. I'll take a turn through the garden, in pity for the pangs of barred affections, even though the king has ordered you not to speak together."

She strolls away.

Imogen cries out in exasperation, "Oh deceitful courtesy! How well this tyrant tickles where she wounds? My dearest husband, I fear my father's anger; but not–as long as I perform my regal duty–what his rage can do to me: you must go; and I shall stay under the hourly gaze of angry eyes, no other reason to live, except that there is this jewel in the world that I may see again."

She breaks down and sobs.

Posthumus says, "My queen: my mistress: Oh lady, no more tears, or I fear I will give cause to be suspected of more tenderness than becomes a man. I will remain the loyalest husband that ever pledged love's allegiance. I'm staying in Rome at one Philario's, who was a friend to my father, known to me only by letters: write to me there, my queen, and with my eyes I will drink the words you send, even if the ink were gall."

They are about to kiss when they hear the Queen return, and break apart.

The Queen says, "Be brief, please: if the king comes, I shall incur I don't know how much of his displeasure."

She stops at the door on her way out to look back, and thinks, "I'll steer him this way: I never do him wrong, but he does accept my injuries to be meant well and pays dearly for my offences."

The Queen walks away into the hall.

Posthumus says, "Only if we were parting for as long as we have yet to live, could this loathness to depart grow any worse. Adieu."

He starts to leave but she restrains him, "No, stay a little longer. If you were just riding out for some air, such a parting is too brief."

She takes a ring from her finger, "Look here, love; this diamond was my mother's: take it, sweetheart; and keep it until you woo another wife, when Imogen is dead."

Posthumus says, "How now? Another? You gentle gods, give me but what I have, and sear off my embraces from another with the promise of death."

He puts on the ring, "Remain, remain here while I have the sense to keep you on. And, sweetest, fairest, just as I accepted your gift, to your infinite loss, so in our trinkets I still win you over."

He takes a bracelet from his wrist, "For my sake wear this. It is a manacle of love; I'll place it upon this fairest prisoner."

He puts the bracelet upon her wrist and slides it along past her elbow until it finally fits halfway to her shoulder.

Imogen says, "Oh dear gods! When shall we meet again?"

King Cymbeline and his Lords enter the gardens.

Posthumus says, "Look out, the king."

Cymbeline sees him and rages, "You base thing, get out of my sight! If after this command you upset our court with your unworthiness, you die. Be gone, you are poison to my blood."

Posthumus bows to Imogen, "May the gods protect you, and bless the good remainders of the court: I am gone."

6.

Posthumus leaves without delay.

Imogen watches him go, "There cannot be a pinch in death sharper than this."

Cymbeline says, "Oh disloyal thing, you should repair my youth, but instead you heap a year's age on me."

Imogen turns to face him, calm, strong and assertive, "I beg you, sir, do not harm yourself with wrath. I am senseless to it. A feeling more exquisite subdues all pangs, all fears."

Cymbeline says, "Past grace? obedience?"

Imogen says, "Past hope, and in despair; in that way I am past grace."

Cymbeline says, "You could have had the sole son of my queen."

Imogen says, "Oh blessed, that I did not: I chose an eagle, and avoided a kite."

Cymbeline says, "You took a beggar; and would have made my throne a seat for baseness."

Imogen says, "No; I rather thought I added a lustre to it."

Cymbeline says, "Oh you vile one!"

Imogen says, "Sir, it's your fault that I love Posthumus: you brought him up as my playfellow, and he is a man worthy of any woman, who overbuys me by almost the amount he pays."

Cymbeline says, "Are you mad?"

Imogen says, "Almost, sir. Jupiter restore me. I wish I were a herdsman's daughter, and my Leonatus our neighbour shepherd's son."

Cymbeline says, "You foolish thing!"

The Queen comes in and he turns his anger on her, "They were together again: you have not followed our command. Away with her, and pen her up."

Imogen cries out.

The Queen says, "Begging your patience. Peace, dear lady daughter, peace. Sweet sovereign, leave us alone; and comfort yourself with your best advice."

Cymbeline storms off with the Lords following, "No, let her lose a drop of blood a day; and die of this folly."

The Queen turns to Imogen, "Shame, you must give way."

She sees Pisanio approach and says, impatiently, "Here is your servant," and addresses him, "Yes? What?"

Pisanio says, "My lord, your son, drew on my master."

The Queen says, "Ha? No harm done, I trust?"

Pisanio says, "There might have been, had my master not toyed with him rather than fought, without the help of anger. They were parted by gentlemen at hand."

The Queen says, "I am so glad."

Imogen says, "Your son is my father's friend; he takes his part. To draw upon an exile. Oh what a noble sir, I wish they were both in the wilderness, myself nearby with a needle, that I might poke the one who steps back."

She turns her attention to Pisanio, "Why have you come from your master?"

8.

Pisanio says, "On his command: he would not let me bring him to the harbour."

He holds up letters, "He left these notes of what commands I should be subject to, when it pleased you to employ me."

The Queen says, "This has been your faithful servant: I would bet my honour he will remain so."

Pisanio says, "I humbly thank your highness."

The Queen addresses Imogen, "Pray, walk with me awhile."

Imogen takes the letters from Pisanio, "I ask about a half-hour before you speak with me," and she turns to to Pisanio, "You shall at least go see my lord on board: for the moment, leave me."

The fuming Queen watches Imogen walk away, reading the letters.

I-2

Cymbeline's palace entrance.

Cloten comes in from outside with two Lords. Cloten is handsome and fighting fit. He wears clothes of the peak of fashion and ostentatious expense.

The First Lord curdles his nose, "Sir, I would advise you to change your shirt; the violence of action has made you reek like a sacrifice: where air comes out, air comes in: there's none so wholesome as what you vent."

Cloten says, "If my shirt were bloody, then I would change it. Did I hurt him?"

The Second Lord keeps his voice low so that only the First Lord hears, "Not so much as his patience."

The First Lord speaks directly to Cloten, with vigour, trying not to laugh at the Second Lord's comments, "Hurt him? His body is a passable carcass, if he isn't hurt: it is a thoroughfare for steel, if it isn't hurt."

The Second Lord speaks lowly, "His steel was in debt; it went out the backside of town."

The First Lord swats the Second Lord.

Cloten says, "The villain would not stand up to me."

The Second Lord says lowly, "No; but he fled forward, toward your face."

The First Lord says, "Stand up to you? You have land enough of your own: but he added to what you have; gave you some ground."

10.

The Second Lord says lowly, "As many inches as you have oceans. Puppy flattery."

Cloten says, "I wish they had not come between us."

The Second Lord says lowly, "So do I, until you had measured how long a fool you were upon the ground."

Cloten says, "And that she should love this fellow and refuse me."

The Second Lord says lowly, "If it is a sin to make a smart choice, she is damned."

The First Lord says, "Sir, as I told you always, her beauty and her brain do not go together: she looks good in a mirror, but I have seen small reflection of her wit."

The Second Lord says lowly, "She does not shine upon fools, in case the reflection should hurt her."

Cloten says, "Come, I'm going to my room. I wish there had been some hurt done."

The Second Lord says lowly, "I wish not, unless it had been the fall of an ass, which is no great hurt."

Cloten says, "You'll go with us?"

The First Lord says, "I'll go with your Lordship."

Cloten addresses the Second Lord, "No, come, let's go together."

The Second Lord says, "Very well, my lord," and reluctantly follows them.

I-3

Imogen's palace suite.

Imogen and Pisanio are seated in the sitting room.

Imogen says, "If only you could reach the shores of the harbour, and question every sail: if he should write and I not get it, it would be a paper lost, as important as a pardon. What was the last thing he said to you?"

Pisanio says, "It was his queen, his queen."

Imogen says, "Then waved his handkerchief?"

Pisanio says, "And kissed it, madam."

Imogen says, "Senseless linen. Happier in that than I: And that was all?"

Pisanio says, "No, madam; for as long as he could make me distinguish him from others, he stayed on deck, with glove, or hat, or handkerchief, still waving to best express how slow his soul sailed on, how swift his ship."

Imogen says, "You should have seen him become as little as a crow, or less, before he vanished."

Pisanio says, "Madam, so I did."

Imogen says, "I would have broken my eye-strings; cracked them, to stay looking, until the diminution of space had pointed him sharp as my needle, no, until he had melted from the smallness of a gnat to air, and then turned my eye and wept. But good Pisanio, when shall we hear from him?"

12.

Pisanio says, "Be assured, madam, at his next opportunity."

Imogen says, "I did not take my proper leave of him. I had pretty things to say: Before I could tell him how I would think about him at certain hours, or could make him swear the women of Italy would not betray my love and his honour, or plan with him, at the sixth hour of morn, at noon, at midnight, to match my prayers with his, for then I am in heaven with him; or before I could give him that parting kiss which I had set between two charmed words, in my father comes and like the tyrannous breath of the north shakes all our buds from growing."

Imogen's Lady approaches, "The queen, madam, desires your highness' company."

Imogen addresses Pisanio, "Those things I asked you to do, do. I will attend the queen."

Pisanio says, "Madam, I shall."

I-4

Rome.

Philario's house.

Philario, Iachimo, a Frenchman, a Dutchman, and a Spaniard are at table gossiping over lunch.

Iachimo says, "Believe it, sir, I met him in Britain: he was on the rise then, expected to prove as worthy as the name he was allowed to use; but I saw him without the help of wonder, though the list of his attributes had been tabled by his side and I could study him by item."

Philario says, "You speak of him when he was less furnished than he is now with that which defines him both without and within."

The Frenchman says, "I met him in France: we had many there who could look at the sun with as firm eyes as he."

Iachimo says, "This matter of marrying his king's daughter, where he must be weighed by her value rather than his own, says a great deal about the matter."

The Frenchman says, "And then his banishment."

Iachimo says, "Yes, and the joining of those under her influence upset at this divorce enhances his reputation; if just to fortify her judgment, which an easy salvo might lay flat otherwise, for taking a beggar without quality. But how does it happen he comes to you? What is the acquaintance?"

Philario says, "His father and I were soldiers together; to whom I have been often bound for no less than my life."

14.

Philario sees Posthumus approach, "Here comes the Briton: let him be entertained amongst you as fitting with gentlemen of your understanding to a stranger of his quality. I beg you all, get to know this gentleman; whom I commend to you as a noble friend of mine: how worthy he is I will tell you later, rather than recount his story in his own hearing."

Posthumus joins them and is seated.

The Frenchman starts up an introductory conversation, "Sir, we spent time together in Orleans."

Posthumus says, "Ever since, I have been indebted to you for courtesies, which I will never be able to repay."

The Frenchman says, "Sir, you over-rate my meager kindness: I was glad I reconciled my countryman and you. It was a pity you were thrust together with such a deadly purpose as each of you bore, upon a matter so slight and trivial in nature."

Posthumus says, "I beg your pardon, sir, I was then a young traveller; rather shy to even agree with what I heard than to be guided by the experience of others: but on my improved judgment–if I don't offend to say it's improved–my quarrel was not altogether slight."

The Frenchman says, "By my faith, yes, to be put to the test of swords, and by such two in all likelihood one would have beaten the other, or both would have fallen."

Iachimo says, "Can we, with manners, ask what the disagreement was?"

Posthumus turns to the food and loads his plate without a word.

The Frenchman fills the void, "Safely, I think: it was a contention in public, which may be publicly reported. It was like an argument we had last night, where each of us fell in praise of our country mistresses;

this gentleman at that time claiming–upon a pledge of blood–his to be more fair, virtuous, wise, chaste, faithful, and less seduceable than any of the rarest of our ladies in France."

Iachimo says, "That lady is not now living, or this gentleman's opinion has worn out by now."

Posthumus says, "She holds her virtue still and I my mind."

Iachimo says, "You must not prefer her so far above ours of Italy."

Posthumus says, "Being provoked as much as I was in France, I would decrease her nothing, though I consider myself to be her worshiper, not her mate."

Iachimo says, "As fair and as good: a kind of hand-in-hand comparison, had been somewhat too fair and too good for any lady in Britain. If she went before others I have seen, as that diamond ring of yours outlustres many I have beheld, I could believe she excelled many: but I have not seen the most precious diamond that is, nor you the lady."

Posthumus says, "I praised her as I rated her: so do I my stone."

Iachimo says, "What do you value it at?"

Posthumus says, "More than the world enjoys."

Iachimo says, "Either your paragon of a mistress is dead, or she's overvalued a trifle."

Posthumus says, "You are mistaken: the one may be sold, or given, if there were wealth enough for the purchase, or merit for the gift: the other is not a thing for sale, and only the gift of the gods."

Iachimo says, "Which the gods have given you?"

16.

Posthumus says, "Which, by their graces, I will keep."

Iachimo says, "You may wear her yours in title but you know strange fowl often land upon neighbouring ponds. Your ring might be stolen: so of your pair of unachievables; one is but frail and the other casual; a cunning thief, or a romancing courtier, would risk winning both."

Posthumus says, "There is none in Italy so accomplished to overcome the honour of my mistress, if, in the holding or loss of that, you term her frail. I do not doubt you have knowledge of thieves; even so, I would not be worried about my ring."

Philario says, "Let us move on, gentlemen."

Posthumus says, "Sir, with all my heart. This worthy signior, I thank him, makes no stranger of me; we are familiar at first."

Iachimo says, "With five times as much conversation, I should gain the ground of your fair mistress, make her give way, even to the yielding, if I had an introduction and opportunity to befriend her."

Posthumus says, "No, no."

Iachimo says, "I dare to put up half of my estate against your ring; which, in my opinion, overvalues it some: but I make my wager against your confidence rather than her reputation: and, to stop you taking offence, I would attempt it against any lady in the world."

Posthumus says, "You are deceived by your belief in bold persuasion; and I don't doubt you'll get what you deserve for your attempt."

Iachimo says, "What's that?"

Posthumus says, "A repulse: though your attempt, as you call it, deserves a punishment too."

Philario says, "Gentlemen, enough of this: it came in too suddenly; let it die as it was born, and, I ask you, get better acquainted."

Iachimo says, "I wish I had put my estate and my neighbour's on the line I spoke of."

Posthumus says, "What lady would you assail?"

Iachimo says, "Yours; whose fidelity you think stands so safe. I will lay you ten thousand ducats to your ring, that, commend me to the court where your lady is, with no more advantage than the opportunity of a second meeting, and I will have that honour of hers which you think is so special."

Posthumus says, "I will wager gold against your gold: my ring I hold dear as my finger; it is part of it."

Iachimo says, "You are her mate and wise: if you buy ladies' flesh even at a million a dram, you can't preserve it from tainting: but I see you have some religion in you, that you fear."

Posthumus says, "This is not just a custom in your tongue: you have a serious purpose, I hope."

Iachimo says, "I am the master of my words, and will do what I have said, I swear."

Posthumus says, "Will you? I shall only lend my diamond until your return: let there be an agreement drawn up between us–my mistress exceeds in goodness the hugeness of your unworthy thinking–I dare you to this match: here's my ring."

He hands it to Iachimo.

Philario intercepts and takes it before Iachimo can react, "I will have it without wagering."

18.

Iachimo says, "By the gods, it is on. If I don't bring you sufficient testimony that I have enjoyed the dearest bodily part of your mistress, my ten thousand ducats are yours; so is your diamond too: if I come away, and leave her in such honour as you have trust in, she your jewel, then this jewel, and my gold are yours: provided I have your permission for my more free entertainment."

Posthumus says, "I accept these conditions; let us have papers drawn between us. Only, you shall answer for this: if you make your voyage upon her and give me directly to understand you have prevailed, I am no longer your enemy; she is not worth our argument. If she remains unseduced, you not making it appear otherwise, for your ill opinion and the assault you have made against her chastity you shall have to answer me with your sword."

Iachimo says, "Your hand."

They shake.

Iachimo says, "A covenant: we will have these things set down by lawyers, and I am straight away for Britain, in case the bargain should catch cold and starve: I'll fetch my gold and have our two wagers recorded."

Posthumus says, "Agreed."

Posthumus and Iachimo go out.

The Frenchman asks, "Will this hold, do you think?"

Philario says, "Signior Iachimo will not back out. Let's follow them."

I-5

The garden of King Cymbeline's palace.

Old Doctor Cornelius waits alone resting on his cane.

The Queen's Ladies enter with the Queen, all tittering about their great errand.

The Queen silences them, "While there is still dew on the ground, gather those flowers; hurry: who has the note?"

The Queen's Lady holds up a scrap of paper, "I, madam."

The Queen says, "Go then."

The Queen's ladies leave and the Queen turns her attention to Cornelius, "Now, master doctor, have you brought those drugs?"

He presents a small box with a skull & crossbones painted on top, "May it please your highness, yes: here they are, madam. But I plead with your grace, without offence–my conscience makes me ask–why you ordered these most poisonous compounds, which are the makers of a languishing death; deadly though slow?"

The Queen says, "I wonder, doctor, why you ask such a question. Haven't I been your pupil for some time? Haven't you taught me how to make perfumes? distil? preserve? so well that our great king himself woos me often for my concoctions? Having proceeded this far–unless you think me devilish–isn't it expected that I increase my knowledge in other methods? I will try the powers of your compounds on the kind of creatures we consider not worth hanging–but none human–to apply antidotes, and that way understand their virtues and effects."

20.

Cornelius says, "Your highness will make your heart hard from this experiment: besides, observing these effects will be offensive and infectious."

The Queen says, "Oh, relax."

Pisanio enters and the Queen thinks, "Here comes a flattering rascal; I will work first upon him: he's loyal to his master, an enemy to my son."

She raises her voice in greeting, "How now, Pisanio?"

And dismisses Cornelius, "Doctor, your services are no longer needed; show yourself out."

She beckons Pisanio, "Listen, a word."

Cornelius steps aside to watch them, thinking, "I don't trust you, madam; but you'll do no harm. I do not like her. She thinks she has exotic lingering poisons: I know her spirit, and won't trust one of her malice with a drug of such damned nature. Those she has will stupefy and dull the sense a while; but there is no danger in its show of death, beyond the locking-up of the spirits for a time, to be refreshed when revived. She is fooled with a false effect; and to be more honest, I must be false with her."

The Queen takes the box to a side table and transfers the contents to another box. She notices Cornelius has not left, "No further service, doctor, until I send for you."

Cornelius says, "I humbly take my leave," and does so.

The Queen disposes of the old box. The contents are now in a box with a lily painted on its top.

She returns her attention to Pisanio, "Does she still weep, what do you say? Don't you think in time she will dry up and let instructions enter where folly reigns? Do your work: when you bring me word she loves my son, I'll tell you on that instant you are as great as your master, greater, because his fortunes can't be spoken for and his name is at its last gasp: he can't return, nor continue where he is: to shift his lodgings is to exchange one misery with another, and every day decays a day's worth in him. What can you expect, to depend on a master that leans, who cannot be built new, nor has no friends, except those willing to prop him up?"

The Queen lets the box fall and Pisanio retrieves it.

The Queen says, "You don't know what you picked up; but take it for your labour: it is something I made, which has five times brought the king back from death: I don't know anything more reviving."

Pisanio hands it back to the Queen but she does not take it, "No, I ask you, take it; it is a sign of a further good that I mean to you. Tell your mistress how the case stands with her; as if it came from yourself. Think what an opportunity you have to change your future. You'll have your mistress still, and my son, who shall take notice of you: I'll convince the king to agree to any manner of advancement you desire; and then myself, chiefly because I urged you to this, I am bound to praise your merits richly.

"Call my women: think on my words."

Pisanio goes into the garden to fetch the Ladies.

The Queen thinks, "A sly and constant rascal, not to be turned; the agent for his master and token link to her lord. If he takes what I gave him it shall unpeople her of ambassadors for her sweetheart, and which she after, unless she changes her nature, shall be assured to taste of too."

22.

Pisanio returns with the Queen's Ladies who have collected many flowers.

The Queen says, "So, so: well done, well done: the violets, cowslips, and the primroses, take to my workroom. Fare well, Pisanio; think on my words."

The Queen and the Queen's Ladies leave.

Pisanio says, "And I shall: but when I prove untrue to my good lord, I'll choke myself: there's all I'll do for you."

I-6

The sitting room in Imogen's suite of the palace.

Imogen sits in front of a shrine of Gods featuring Jupiter, adjusting her crown, prepping for court, "A cruel father, and a false stepmother; a foolish suitor to a wedded lady, whose husband is banished: Oh, that husband, my supreme crown of grief, and these renewed irritations of it. If only I had been kidnapped, like my two brothers, I'd be happy: but most doomed to disappointment is the desire that is too glorious: blessed be those, however humble, that have what they want, which gives spice to comfort."

Pisanio enters with Iachimo.

Imogen says, "Who may this be? Not now."

Pisanio says, "Madam, a noble gentleman of Rome, comes from my lord with letters."

Her whole impatient manner changes to eager welcome.

Iachimo bows in greeting, "You blush, madam? The worthy Leonatus is in safety and greets your highness dearly."

He presents a letter.

Imogen takes it eagerly, "Thanks, good sir: you are kindly welcome."

She turns the letter to the shrine for a moment then breaks the seal and opens it.

24.

Iachimo thinks as he watches her, "From the outside all of her is most rich: If she has a mind just as extraordinary, she is the rarest exotic bird, and I have lost the wager. Boldness be my friend: Arm me, audacity, from head to foot, or like the Parthian warrior, I shall avoid a fight by fleeing."

Imogen reads part of the letter out loud, "'He is one of the noblest note, to whose kindnesses I am most infinitely tied. Reflect upon him accordingly, as you value your truest Leonatus.'"

She looks up from the letter, "That's as far as I will read aloud: but the centre of my heart is warmed by the rest, and takes it thankfully. You are as welcome–worthy sir–as I have words to offer you, and shall find it so in all that I can do."

She continues reading the letter.

Iachimo says, "Thanks, fairest lady," and then steps back, boldly eyeing her body as he speaks, "What, are men mad? has nature given them eyes to see this vaulted arch, and the rich crop of sea and land, which can distinguish between the fiery orbs above and the twinned stones upon the endless beach? and can't make the distinction between fair and foul with eyes so precious?"

Imogen says, "What causes your amazement?"

Iachimo continues without answering, "It cannot be in the eye, for apes and monkeys between two such females would chatter with this one and scorn the other; nor in the judgment, for even an idiot in this case of beauty would be wisely definite; nor in the appetite; sluttishness opposed by such fine excellence would make desire dry heave, not so tempted to feed."

Imogen says, "Good heavens, what is the matter?"

Iachimo says, "The addicted try to satisfy unquenchable desires, that tub filled and still running, feasting first on the lamb, longs after the garbage."

Imogen says, "What, dear sir, moves you so? Are you well?"

Iachimo says, "Thanks, madam; well."

He gestures to Pisanio, "I beg you, sir, go to my servant's quarters where I left him: he is temperamental in strange places."

Pisanio looks at Imogen to be sure it's alright to leave her alone with this oddball. Imogen nods her assent.

Pisanio says, "I was going, sir, to give him welcome," and leaves.

Imogen says, "My lord is well? His health, I beg you?"

Iachimo says, "Well, madam."

Imogen says, "Is he disposed to mirth? I hope he is."

Iachimo says, "Exceeding pleasant; there isn't a stranger there who is more merry and more gamesome: he is called the Briton reveller."

Imogen says, "When he was here, he was inclined to sadness, often without knowing why."

Iachimo says, "I never saw him sad. There is a Frenchman, his companion, an eminent monsieur, that loves a girl at home; he burns with thick sighs while the jolly Briton–your lord, I mean–laughs from deep within, cries 'Oh, can my sides hold, to think that any man, who knows by history, report, or his own experience, what a woman is, yes, what she can't help but be, will give up his freedom for assured bondage?'"

Imogen says, "Did my lord say so?"

26.

Iachimo says, "Yes, madam, shedding tears of laughter: it is quite fun to hear him mock the Frenchman. But the heavens know some men are just as much to blame."

Imogen says, "Not him, I hope."

Iachimo protests too easily, "Not him: yet heaven's bounty might be used more thankfully. In himself, it is much; in you, which I consider his beyond all limits, while I am bound to envy, I am bound to pity too."

Imogen says, "What do you pity, sir?"

Iachimo says, "Two creatures heartily."

Imogen says, "Am I one, sir? You look on me: what ruin do you see in me that deserves your pity?"

Iachimo says, "I can't say it: To end up hidden from the radiant sun and happiness in a dungeon for spite?"

Imogen understands. She removes her crown and sets it down, then turns back to him, "I ask you, sir, deliver with more openness your answers. Why do you pity me?"

Iachimo says, "That others do–I was about to say–enjoy your–but it is the duty of the gods to avenge it, not mine to speak about it."

Imogen says, "You seem to know something of me, or what concerns me: I ask you–since worrying that things are bad often hurts more than being sure they are; because certainties are either past remedies, or, knowing in time provides the remedy–tell me what you both push and pull."

Iachimo says, "If only I had this cheek to bathe my lips upon; this hand, whose touch, whose every touch, would force the feeler's soul to an oath of loyalty; this object, which steals the wild motion of my eye, fixing it only here.

"Would I slobber over lips as worn as the stairs that mount the Capitol; join with hands made hard with hourly falsehoods–falsehood being their job–then giving sidelong glances with an eye as clouded as smoky light fed with stinking tallow; it were fit that all the plagues of hell should at one time encounter such unfaithfulness."

Imogen says, "My lord, I fear, has forgot Britain."

Iachimo says, "And himself. I would not, knowing this, express the baseness of his change; but it is your grace that charms this report from my mutest conscience to my tongue."

Imogen says, "Let me hear no more."

Iachimo says, "Oh dearest soul: your cause strikes my heart with pity, that makes me sick. A lady so fair, and fastened to an empire, would make the greatest king double, to be partnered with harlots hired with that same allowance which your own bank account makes possible: with diseased players that risk all their infirmities for gold which rottenness can lend nature. Such boiled tarts that might poison poison: be revenged; or she that bore you was no queen, and you defy your great lineage."

Imogen says, "Revenged: how should I be revenged? If this is true–since I have such a love that my ears must not denounce in haste–if it is true, how should I be revenged?"

Iachimo says, "If he made me live like Diana's priest, between cold sheets, while he vaults a variety of ramps in spite of you, spreading your money? Revenge it. I dedicate myself to your sweet pleasure, more noble than that traitor to your bed, and will continue constant to your affection, still secret as loyal."

28.

Imogen calls, "What ho, Pisanio?"

Iachimo says, "Let me offer my service on your lips."

He tries to move in for a kiss.

Imogen says, "Away, I condemn my ears that have listened to you so long. If you were honourable, you would have told this tale for virtue, not for such an end you seek–as common as strange. You wrong a gentleman, who is as far from your report as you are from honour, and solicit a lady that despises you and the devil equally.

"What ho, Pisanio?

"The king my father shall be made acquainted of your assault: if he thinks it fit that an insolent stranger to his court does his business like he was in a Roman stew house and reveal his beastly thoughts to us, he has a court he little cares for and a daughter he doesn't respect at all.

"What ho, Pisanio?"

Iachimo hasn't a clue what to do. All is lost, then suddenly he claps his hands in joy and smiles sweetly at Imogen who is taken aback by his response.

Iachimo says, "Oh happy Leonatus I may say, the faith that your lady has of you deserves your trust, and your most perfect goodness her assured credit. Blessed live you long, a lady to the worthiest sir that any country called his; and you his mistress, for the worthiest fit.

"Give me your pardon. I have said this to know if your affections were deeply rooted; and shall make your lord, that which he is, new over: and he is the truest mannered; a wizard that enchants societies; half all men's hearts are his."

Imogen begins to calm, "You make amends."

Iachimo says, "He sits among men like a god descended: he has a kind of honour that sets him apart, seeming more than a mortal. Don't be angry, most mighty princess, that I ventured to get you to believe a false report; which has honoured with confirmation your great judgment in the choice of a sir so rare, who you know cannot be untrue: the love I have for him compelled me to fan you like that, but the gods made you, unlike all others, unachievable. I beg your pardon."

Imogen says, "All is well, sir: take my power in the court for yours."

Iachimo says, "My humble thanks. I almost forgot to ask of your grace a small request, and yet of importance too, because it concerns your lord. Myself and other noble friends are partners."

Imogen says, "Please, what is it?"

Iachimo says, "Some dozen of us Romans and your lord–the best feather of our wing–have pooled money to buy a present for the emperor which I, the buyer for the rest, have done in France: it is plate of rare design, and jewels of rich and exquisite form; all of great value; and I am concerned, being a stranger, to have them safely stored: may it please you to take them in protection?"

Imogen says, "Willingly; and pledge my honour for their safety: since my lord has interest in them, I will keep them in my bedchamber."

Iachimo has trouble not grinning, "They are in a trunk, attended by my men: I will make bold to send them to you, only for this night; I must embark tomorrow."

Imogen says, "Oh, no, no."

Iachimo says, "Yes, I must; or I'll short my word by lengthening my return. I crossed the seas from France on purpose and on promise to see your grace."

30.

Imogen says, "I thank you for your pains: but not away tomorrow."

Iachimo says, "Oh, I must, madam: therefore if you want to greet your lord with writing, do it tonight: I am running late which is related to the offering of our present."

Imogen says, "I will write. Send your trunk to me; it shall be kept safe, and returned truly."

Iachimo bows his thanks.

Imogen says, "You're very welcome."

II-1

Cymbeline's palace entrance.

Cloten and the two Lords come in.

Cloten says, "Was there ever man had such luck? when my bowl kissed the jack, to be hit away on the next throw? I had a hundred pound on it. And then a whoreson traitor confronts me for swearing; as if I borrowed my oaths from him and might not spend them at my pleasure."

The First Lord says, "What did he gain by it? You broke his head with your bowl."

The Second Lord speaks lowly so that only the First Lord hears, "If his wit had been like him that broke it, it would have run all out."

Cloten says, "When a gentleman is disposed to swear, it is not for any standers-by to curtail his oaths, ha?"

The Second Lord says, "No, my lord," adding lowly, "nor crop the ears of them."

Cloten says, "Whoreson dog. I give him satisfaction? I wish he had been one of my rank."

The Second Lord says lowly, "To have smelt like a fool."

Cloten says, "I am not upset more at any thing in the world: curse it. I'd rather not be nobility; they dare not fight with me, because of the queen my mother: every Jack-slave gets his bellyful of fighting, and I must go up and down like a cock that nobody can match."

The Second Lord says lowly, "You are cock and capon too; and you crow, cock, with your comb on."

32.

Cloten says, "What did you say?"

The Second Lord says, "It is not fit your lordship should have to give satisfaction to every fellow that you give offence to."

Cloten says, "No, I know that." He approaches the Second Lord, "but it is fit I should commit offence to my inferiors."

The Second Lord says, "Yes, it is fit for your lordship only."

Cloten says, "That's what I said."

The First Lord says, "Did you hear of a stranger that's come to court tonight?"

Cloten says, "A stranger, and I don't know about it?"

The Second Lord says lowly, "He's a strange fellow himself, and doesn't know it."

The First Lord says, "There's an Italian come; and, it is thought, one of Leonatus' friends."

Cloten rants, "Leonatus? A banished rascal; and he's another, whoever he is. Who told you of this stranger?"

The First Lord says, "One of your lordship's pages."

Cloten says, "Is it proper if I go to look at him? is there no loss of dignity in it?"

The Second Lord says, "You cannot lose your dignity, my lord."

Cloten says, "Not easily, I think."

The Second Lord says lowly, "You are a fool granted; therefore your deeds being foolish, do not lose your dignity."

Cloten says, "Come, I'll go see this Italian: what I have lost today at bowls I'll win tonight from him. Come, go."

The Second Lord says, "I'll follow in a minute your lordship."

Cloten leaves with the First Lord.

The Second Lord thinks, "That such a crafty devil as his mother should yield the world this ass: a woman that bears all others down with her brain; and her son can't subtract two from twenty, for his life, and leave eighteen. Alas, poor princess, divine Imogen, the things you endure, between a father governed by your step-mother, a mother who is hourly hatching plots, a wooer more hateful than one of your dear husband's farts. Then that horrid act of divorce, he wants to make the heavens hold firm the walls of your dear honour. Keep unshaked that temple, your fair mind, that you may enjoy your banished lord and this great land."

II-2

Imogen's bedroom is hung with tapestries of silk and silver thread. The most prominent is of Cleopatra arriving on her barge to meet Anthony. The chimney-piece is a sculpture of Diana, Goddess of the hunt, bathing. Two silver cupids serve as andirons and there are golden cherubs decorating the roof.

A large travelling trunk has been pushed into one corner.

Imogen is in bed, reading.

Imogen's Lady comes in with towels.

Imogen says, "Who's there? my woman Helen?"

Imogen's Lady says, "At your pleasure, madam."

Imogen says, "What time is it?"

Imogen's Lady says, "Almost midnight, madam."

Imogen says, "I have read three hours then: my eyes are tired: fold the page where I left off: to bed: don't take the candle away, leave it burning; and if you can wake by four, call me. Sleep has seized me wholly."

Imogen's Lady leaves.

Imogen sits up in her bed and prays to a shrine of gods, "To your protection I commend myself, gods. I ask you to guard me from demons and the tempters of the night."

She lays back down and kisses the bracelet before settling in to sleep.

*

After she falls asleep the trunk lid opens and Iachimo slithers out into the shadows.

He observes that all is quiet, "The crickets sing, and man's overworked sense repairs itself with rest. The rapist Tarquin snuck across the floor before he woke the chastity he stole."

He approaches the bed and gazes at Imogen's sleeping form, "Venus, how nobly you dignify your bed, fresh lily, and whiter than the sheets: that I might touch."

He tries but hasn't the courage to touch her, "But kiss; one kiss."

He cautiously touches his lips, barely, to hers, "Rubies unparalleled, how dearly they do it: it is her breathing that perfumes the room: the candle flame bows toward her, and would peep under her lids, to see the lights now curtained under these windows, white and azure, laced with heaven's own blue."

He breaks away from her and looks around the room. He takes out a fold of paper and a pencil stub, "But to my plan, to note the room: I will write all down: such and such pictures; there the window; such the adornment of her bed; the tapestry figures, the contents of its story."

His attention drifts again to her sleeping form, "Ah, but some natural notes about her body will do more than ten thousand lesser proofs to enrich my inventory. Oh sleep, you mimic of death, lie heavy upon her, and keep her like a chapel monument."

He spots the bracelet Posthumus gave her and grabs at it to take it off her arm, "Come off, come off: as tricky as the Gordian knot."

Finally it comes off and he pockets it.

36.

"It is mine; and this will prove outwardly, as strongly as the conscience does within, to the maddening of her lord."

He reaches again to touch her bare skin but can't bring himself to do it. Instead he gingerly plucks the sheet and lifts it to uncover her breast.

"A five-pointed mole on her left breast, like the crimson drops in the bottom of a cowslip: here's the proof, stronger than any law could make: this secret will force him to think I have picked the lock and taken the treasure of her honour."

Imogen stirs and pulls the covers.

Iachimo lets go, "No more. To what end? Why should I write down what is riveted, screwed to my memory?"

He notices the book at her bedside, "She has been reading the tale of cruel Tereus; here the page is turned down where Philomela gave up.

He crosses to the corner and takes a quick look around, "I have enough: to the trunk again. Swift, swift, you dragons of the night, that dawn may bare the raven's eye: I hide in fear. Though this is a heavenly angel, hell is here."

He climbs back inside the trunk as the clock strikes.

"One, two, three: time, time."

On the fourth stroke he shuts the lid.

Imogen's Lady enters to wake her.

II-3

An ante-chamber leading to Imogen's suite.

Cloten and the First Lord arrive in front of the door.

The First Lord says, "Your lordship is the most patient man in loss, the coldest that ever turned up an ace."

Cloten says, "It would make any man cold to lose."

The First Lord says, "But not every man patient after the noble temper of your lordship. You are most hot and furious when you win."

Cloten says, "Winning gives any man courage. If I could win this foolish Imogen, I should have gold enough. It's almost morning, isn't it?"

The First Lord says, "Day, my lord."

Cloten says, "I wish this music would get here: I was advised to give her music in the morning; they say it will touch the heart."

Three Musicians arrive, Guitar, Fiddle, and a Singer.

Cloten hurries them, "Come on, tune."

They warm themselves and their instruments as he continues, "If you can touch her heart with your fingering, well and good; we'll try with tongue too: if none will do, let her be; but I'll never give up."

The Musicians face him, ready. Cloten says, "First, a very excellent good-conceited thing; after, a wonderful sweet air, with admirable rich words to it: and then let her contemplate."

He gestures. The Singer sings accompanied by the Guitar and Fiddle.

38.

"Hark, hark, the lark at heaven's gate sings,
And Phoebus 'gins arise,
His steeds to water at those springs
On chaliced flowers that lies;
And winking Mary-buds begin
To ope their golden eyes:
With every thing that pretty is,
My lady sweet, arise:
Arise, arise."

When they finish Cloten waits only a moment, then, "So, get out. If this touched her heart, I will reward your music the better: if not, it is a fault of her ears, which horse-hairs and calves'-guts, nor the voice of a eunuch to boot, can mend."

The three Musicians leave.

The First Lord sees the Royals approaching, "Here comes the king."

Cloten says, "I am glad I was up so late; for that's the reason I am up so early: he cannot choose but take this service I have done fatherly."

King Cymbeline and the Queen join Cloten who greets them, "Good morning to your majesty and to my gracious mother."

Cymbeline says, "Are you waiting here at the door of our stern daughter? Won't she come out?"

Cloten says, "I have serenaded her with music, but she chooses not to notice."

Cymbeline says, "The exile of her favourite is too new; she has not yet forgot him: more time must wear the print of his remembrance out, and then she's yours."

The Queen says, "You owe a lot to the king, who doesn't let a chance go by to praise you to his daughter. Adapt yourself to orderly soliciting, and be friendly according to the occasion; make her denials increase your services as if inspired to do those duties which you offer her; that in all you obey her, except when she commands your dismissal of which you are senseless."

Cloten overreacts to the word, "Senseless? Not so."

A Messenger appears at the King's side and kneels. The King gestures. The Messenger reports, "If it please you, sir, ambassadors from Rome; the one is Caius Lucius."

Cymbeline says, "A worthy fellow, although he comes on an angry purpose but that's not his fault: we must receive him according to the honour of his sender; his goodness we already know, we must grant our attention."

He and the Queen prepare to leave.

Cymbeline addresses Cloten, "Our dear son, when you have said good morning to your mistress, attend the queen and us; we shall have need to employ you towards this Roman. Come, our queen."

Cloten says, "If she is up, I'll speak with her; if not, let her lie still and dream."

The entourage goes out leaving him alone.

He knocks at the door, "By your leave, hello.

He takes out a coin purse, "I know her women are about her: what if I line one of their hands? it is gold which often buys admittance and makes even Diana's rangers false, yielding the game to the poacher. It is gold which kills the honest man and saves the thief; or sometime hangs both. What can't it do or undo? I will make one of her women counsel to me, because I still don't understand the case myself."

40.

He knocks again, harder, "By your leave."

The door opens and Imogen's Lady appears, "Who knocks?"

Cloten says, "A gentleman."

Imogen's Lady says, "No more?"

Cloten says, "Yes, a gentlewoman's son."

Imogen's Lady says, "That's more than some whose tailors are as expensive as yours, can boast of. What's your lordship's pleasure?"

Cloten says, "Your lady's person: is she ready?"

Imogen's Lady says, "Yes, to keep her chamber."

Cloten offers a handful of coins, "There is gold for you; sell me your good report."

Imogen's Lady doesn't look at the coins, "How, my good name? or to speak of you what I think is good?"

She hears a sound behind her and bows out, "The princess."

Imogen appears and sees his offering.

Cloten pockets the coins, "Good morning, fairest, sister, your sweet hand."

Imogen says, "Good morning, sir. You go to too much pain to buy anything but trouble; the thanks I give is to tell you that I am poor of thanks and scarce can spare them."

Cloten says, "Still, I swear I love you."

Imogen says, "If you just said it, it would make the same impression: if you swear still, your payment is still that I disregard it."

Cloten says, "This is no answer."

Imogen says, "I would not speak except so you can't say I yield by being silent. I ask you, spare me: in faith, I shall unfold equal discourtesy to your best kindness: one of your great knowing should have learned restraint when it was taught."

Cloten says, "To leave you in your madness would be my sin: I will not."

Imogen says, "Fools do not cure mad folks."

Cloten overreacts to the word, "Do you call me fool?"

Imogen says, "Since I'm mad, I do: if you'll be patient, I'll not be mad; that cures both of us. I'm sorry, sir, you make me forget a lady's manners, by being so outspoken: and learn now, for all time, that I, who know my heart, do here pronounce, the very truth of it, I don't care for you, and am so near the lack of charity–to accuse myself–I hate you; which I'd rather you felt than make it my boast."

Cloten says, "You sin against obedience, which you owe your father. The contract you pretend with that base wretch, one brought up on charity, an orphan raised on scraps of the court, it is no contract, none: and though it is accepted by commoner parties–and who is more common than he?–to join their souls, with no more obligation than brats and poverty, in their self-tied knot: you are restrained from that freedom by the consequence of the crown, and must not stain the precious distinction of it with a base slave. A good for nothing fit for livery, servant coat, or pantry apron, not so eminent."

42.

Imogen says, "Depraved fellow if you were the son of Jupiter and nothing more besides what you are, you are too low to be his groom: you would only be dignified enough to the point of envy, if according to your virtues, to be given the title of under hangman of his kingdom, and hated for being promoted so well."

Cloten says, "May the south-fog rot him."

Imogen says, "He can never meet more bad fortune than has come to be with your name on it. His simplest garment, that has only ever brushed his body, is dearer in my respect than all the hairs on your head, even if they were all men like you."

She calls, "How now, Pisanio?"

Cloten says, "His garment? Now the devil."

Pisanio comes in and Imogen addresses him, "Go to my woman Dorothy immediately–"

Cloten says, "His garment?"

Imogen dismisses Cloten's raving, "I am haunted by a fool, frightened, and angered worse.

"Go ask my woman to look for a jewel that has left my arm: it was your master's. Curse me if I would lose it for the riches of any king in Europe. I think I saw it this morning: I'm sure it was on my arm last night. I kissed it: I hope it is not gone, to have to tell my lord that I kiss nothing but he."

Pisanio says, "It will not be lost."

Imogen says, "I hope not: go and search."

Pisanio leaves and Cloten says, "You have abused me: his simplest garment?"

Imogen says, "Yes, I said so, sir: if you want to make something of it call for witnesses."

Cloten says, "I will inform your father."

Imogen says, "Your mother too: she's my good friend, and will think, I expect, the worst of me. So, I leave you, sir, to the worst of discontent."

She closes the door in his face.

Cloten says, "I'll be revenged: 'His simplest garment?' Well."

II-4

Rome. Philario's house. The same group–the Spaniard, the Frenchman, and the Dutchman–are gathered for lunch.

Posthumus and Philario sit across from each other. On the table before them is the contract, the ring and the gold.

Posthumus who has been staring blankly at the ring, looks up and addresses Philario, "Don't worry, sir: I wish I was so sure to win the king as I am confident her honour will remain hers."

Philario says, "What approaches do you make to him?"

Posthumus says, "None, just to endure until the change of time, shiver in the present winter's state and wish that warmer days would come. In these burning hopes, I barely justify your help. If it fails I will die in your debt."

Philario says, "Your very goodness and your company overpays all I do for you.

"By now, your king has heard from great Augustus: Caius Lucius will do his commission thoroughly: and I think he'll grant the tribute, send the overdue funds, before he will face our Romans, whose memory is still fresh in their grief."

Posthumus says, "Although I'm not a statesman, nor likely to be, I believe that this will prove a war; and you shall hear the legions stationed in France land in our brave Britain before there is news of any penny tribute being paid. Our countrymen are more organized than when Julius Caesar smiled at their lack of skill, but found their courage worthy of his frowns: their discipline, now winged with their courage, will make known to those who try them they are such people that shape the world."

Iachimo is shown in.

Philario says, "See Iachimo."

Posthumus says, "The swiftest hooves have sped you by land; and favourable winds kissed your sails, to make your vessel nimble."

Philario says, "Welcome, sir."

Posthumus says, "I hope the briefness of your answer made the speediness of your return."

Iachimo says, "Your lady is one of the prettiest that I have looked upon."

Posthumus says, "And therefore the best; or let her beauty sit in a window to tempt false hearts and be false with them."

Iachimo says, "Here are letters for you."

Posthumus says, "Their tone is good, I trust."

Iachimo says, "Very likely."

Philario asks, "Was Caius Lucius in the British court when you were there?"

Iachimo says, "He was expected, but not there."

Posthumus says, "All is well yet."

Posthumus notices Iachimo staring at the ring, "Does this stone sparkle as it should? or isn't it too dull for your wearing?"

Iachimo says, "If I had lost it, I should have lost the worth of it in gold as well. I'll make a journey twice as far, to enjoy a second night of such sweet shortness which was mine in Britain, for the ring is won."

46.

Posthumus jokes, "The stone is too hard to come by."

Iachimo says, "Not a bit, your lady being so easy."

Posthumus grows serious, "Sir, do not make sport of your loss. I hope you know that we must not continue friends."

Iachimo says, "Good sir, we must, if you keep your word. Had I not brought the knowledge of your mistress home, I agree we were to quarrel further: but I claim myself the winner of her honour, together with your ring; and not the wronger of her or you, having proceeded according to both your wills."

Posthumus says, "If you can prove that you have tasted her in bed, my hand and ring are yours. If not, the foul opinion you had of her pure honour gains or loses your sword or mine, or masterless leaves both to whoever finds them."

Iachimo says, "Sir, my details, being so near the truth as I will make them, must first convince you: whose strength I will confirm with an oath; which, I doubt you will make me take, when you find you don't need it."

With trepidation Posthumus says, "Proceed."

Iachimo says, "First, her bedchamber," he plays to the others with a sly grin, "–where, I confess, I didn't sleep, but declare I had that which was well worth keeping awake for–it was hanged with tapestry of silk and silver; images of proud Cleopatra, when she met her Roman, and the river Cydnus swelled above the banks, or for the press of boats or pride: a piece of work so admirably done, so rich, that it competed in workmanship and value; and I wondered how could it be so rarely and exactly wrought, since the true life on it was–"

Impatiently Posthumus interrupts, "This is true; and you might have heard this here, by me, or someone else."

Iachimo says, "More particulars must justify my knowledge."

Posthumus says, "They must, or do your honour injury."

Iachimo glances at his notes, "The chimney is at the south of the chamber, and the chimney-piece of chaste Diana bathing: never have I seen figures so lifelike: the cutter was as skilled as nature; without motion and breath."

Posthumus says, "This is a thing which you might also learn from relationships. It is much spoken of."

Iachimo knows he is getting to Posthumus and lays on another layer of deco admiration, "The roof of the chamber is fretted with golden cherubs: her andirons–I had forgot them–were two winking cupids of silver, each standing on one foot, nicely hanging from their brands."

Posthumus urges him, "This is about her honour: Let it be granted you have seen all this–and praise to your memory–the description of what is in her chamber does not save the wager you have laid."

Iachimo says, "Then, if you can stay calm, I ask permission to show this jewel."

He shows the bracelet.

"See." He pockets the bracelet, "And now it is gone again: it must be married to your diamond; I'll keep them."

Posthumus says, "By Jupiter. Let me see it again: is that the bracelet I left with her?"

Iachimo shows the bracelet again, keeping it out of reach, tantalizing Posthumus by mimicking the actions of his words, "Sir–I thank her–that: she stripped from her arm; I can see her now; her pretty movement was worth more than her gift, and yet enhanced it too: she gave it to me, and said she prized it once."

48.

Posthumus, bewildered, grasps for an explanation, "Maybe she took it off to send to me."

Iachimo gestures at the letter, "She writes that to you, does she?"

Posthumus is devastated, "Oh, no, no, no, it is true. Here, take this too; it is a dagger to my eye, it kills me to look at it."

He knocks the ring at Iachimo who pockets it quickly.

Posthumus says, "There is no honour where there is beauty. Truth, where there is show. Love, where there is another man: the vows of women have no more meaning wherever they are made, than their virtues; which are none: Oh, false beyond measure."

Philario says, "Patience, sir, and take your ring again; it is not yet won: maybe she lost it; or who knows maybe one of her women, being bribed, has stolen it from her?"

Desperately Posthumus grasps at the idea, "Very true; and, I hope that's how he came by it. Give back my ring: give me some solid sign about her, more evident than this; for this was stolen."

Iachimo reacts indignantly upset. He takes the ring out and offers it back, "By Jupiter, I had it from her arm."

Posthumus backs away horrified, "Did you hear? He swears: by Jupiter he swears. It's true, keep the ring, it's true: I am sure she would not lose it: her ladies are all sworn and honourable: they convinced to steal it? And by a stranger? No, he has enjoyed her: she has bought the name of whore dearly. There, take your winnings; and divide it with the fiends of hell."

Philario says, "Sir, be patient: this is not strong enough to be believed of one persuaded well of–"

Posthumus interrupts bluntly, "Never talk about it; she has been colted by him."

Iachimo addresses Philario, although really talking to Posthumus, "If you seek further satisfaction. Under her breast–worth pressing–lies a mole, right thrilled I was about that most delicate placement: by my life, I kissed it; and it made me hungry to feed again, though full. You remember this stain upon her?"

Posthumus sinks into despair, "Yes, and it confirms another stain, as big as hell can hold, if there is no more except it."

Iachimo says, "Will you hear more?"

Posthumus says, "Spare your arithmetic: never count the turns; once is the same as a million."

Iachimo says, "I'll be sworn–"

Posthumus angrily interrupts, "No swearing! If you swear you haven't done it, you lie. I will kill you if you deny you made me a cuckold."

Iachimo says, "I'll deny nothing."

Posthumus says, "Oh, if I had her here, I'd tear her limb from limb: I will go there and do it, in the court, in front of her father. I'll do something–" He leaves in a flurry.

Philario says, "Quite beyond the control of patience. You have won: let's follow him, and calm this hate he has toward himself."

Iachimo says, "With all my heart."

II-5

Posthumus's room in Philario's house.

Posthumus paces, "Is there no way for men to be but women must control half of us? We are all bastards; and that most esteemed man I called my father, was I don't know where when I was stamped; some coiner with his tools made me a counterfeit: yet my mother seemed the Diana of that time as does my wife the ideal of this.

"Oh, vengeance, vengeance! She restrained me from my husband's pleasure and pleaded with me often to be patient. She did it with a modesty so rosy it might well have warmed old Saturn; that I thought her as chaste as unsunned snow. Oh, all the devils! This yellow Iachimo, in an hour–wasn't it?–or less–at first? maybe he didn't speak, but, like a full-acorned wild boar, cried oh, and mounted her; found no opposition from where he expected it and she should guard.

"If I could find the woman's part in me, for there's no impulse that tends to vice in man that isn't the woman's part: if it's lying, note it, the woman's; flattering, hers; deceiving, hers; lust and rank thoughts, hers, hers; revenges, hers; ambitions, covetings, changeable pride, disdain, affected longing, slanders, moodiness, all faults that can be named, no, that hell knows, hers, in part or all; but rather, all; for they are not even constant to vice but change one vice, a minute old, for one not half so old. I'll denounce them, detest them, curse them: in true hate it is smarter to pray they get their wish: the very devils cannot plague them better."

III-1

The court hall of Cymbeline's palace.

Dressed in state robes, King Cymbeline, the Queen, Cloten, and the Lords settle in.

The Queen sits to one side of the King but the Princess's chair, on the other side, is empty. The Queen gestures and Cloten sits there.

The King waves his hand and Caius Lucius and his attendants are shown in.

Cymbeline says, "Now say, what does Augustus Caesar want with us?"

Caius Lucius says, "When Julius Caesar–whose memory still lives in men's eyes and will be theme and hearing ever to ears and tongues–was in this Britain and conquered it, Cassibelan, your uncle–famous in Caesar's praises, not a bit less than his feats deserved–for himself and his successors granted Rome a yearly tribute of three thousand pounds, which lately you have left unpaid."

The Queen says, "And, to end the mystery, shall always be."

Cloten says, "There will be many Caesars before another like Julius. Britain is a world by itself; and we will pay nothing for wearing our own noses."

The Queen says, "That opportunity which then they had to take from us, we have again. Remember, sir, my liege, the kings your ancestors, together with the natural bastion of your isle, which stands as Neptune's park, ribbed and enclosed with unscalable rocks and roaring waters, with sands that will not support your enemies' boats, sucking them up to the topmast. Caesar made a kind of conquest here; but didn't make his brag of 'came' and 'saw' and 'conquered': with shame–that first time he ever touched here–he was carried off from our coast, twice beaten; and his ships–poor pilotless baubles–were tossed like eggshells on our terrible seas, and cracked as easily against our rocks: for the joy of it the famed Cassibelan, who was once at the point–oh fickle fortune–of master Caesar's sword, made London-town bright with rejoicing fires and Britons strut with courage."

Cloten says, "There's no more tribute to be paid: our kingdom is stronger than it was then. And, as I said, there are no more such Caesars: some of them may have crooked noses, but we owe such straight-armed beggars, nothing."

Cymbeline says, "Son, let your mother finish."

The Queen gestures to have Cloten speak for her.

Cloten says, "We have many among us can grip as hard as Cassibelan: I do not say I am one; but I have some skill. Why should we pay tribute? If Caesar can hide the sun from us with a blanket, or put the moon in his pocket, we will pay him tribute for light; otherwise, sir, ask for no more tribute."

Cymbeline says, "You must know, until the unjust Romans extorted this tribute from us, we were free: Caesar's ambition, which swelled so much that it almost stretched the sides of the world, against all reason put the yoke upon us. To shake it off fits a warlike people, which we reckon ourselves to be."

Cloten says, "We do."

Cymbeline says, "Tell Caesar, our ancestor was Mulmutius who ordained our laws, whose use Caesar's sword has mangled; whose repair and promotion shall, by the power we hold, be our good deed, though it angers Rome. Mulmutius made our laws. He was the first of Britain to put his brows within a golden crown and call himself a king."

Caius Lucius says, "I'm sorry, Cymbeline, that I pronounce Augustus Caesar–Caesar, that has more kings as his servants than you have domestic officers–your enemy: receive it from me, then: war and confusion in Caesar's name I pronounce against you: expect a fury that cannot be resisted."

He relaxes a little of his formal manner, "Therefore defied, I thank you for myself."

Cymbeline says, "You are welcome, Caius. Your Caesar knighted me. I spent much of my youth under him; from him I gathered honour; which if he would seek it of me again, it is appropriate I keep it to the death. I am informed that the Pannonians and Dalmatians are now up in arms for their liberties; not to consider such a precedent would show the Britons cold: Caesar shall not find them so."

Caius Lucius says, "Let proof speak."

Cymbeline gestures to Cloten, who says, "His majesty bids you welcome. Stay with us a day or two, or longer: if you look for us afterwards on other terms, you'll find us in our salt-water girdle: if you beat us out of it, it's yours; if you fall in the adventure, our crows shall feast the better for you; and there's an end."

Caius Lucius says, "So be it, sir."

Cymbeline says, "I know your master's pleasure and he mine: all that remains is 'Welcome.'"

He waves his hand and food is served.

III-2

Pisanio is alone in the sitting room of Imogen's suite.

He holds an open letter from Posthumus containing another envelope. He has just read the letter meant for him, "How? of adultery? Why didn't you write what monster accused her? Oh master, what strange infection fell into your ear? What poison-tongued Italian persuaded your too accepting hearing? Disloyal? No. She is punished for her truth, and undergoes, more goddess-like than wife-like, assaults that would destroy some more virtuous. Oh, my master, your mind is as low to her now as your fortunes. How? That I should murder her, upon the love and truth and vows which I have made to obey your command? I her? Her blood? If that is how to do good service, never let me be counted serviceable. How do I look, that I should seem to lack humanity so much as this fact comes to?"

He reads, "'Do it: the letter that I have sent her, by her own command shall give you the opportunity.'"

He stares at the sealed envelope, "Oh damned paper, black as the ink that's on you: Senseless bauble, are you an accomplice in this act, and look so virgin-like on the outside?"

Imogen enters and Pisanio thinks, "Hello, here she comes. I am ignorant of what I am commanded."

Imogen sees he has letters and approaches him, "How now, Pisanio?"

Pisanio hands her the unopened envelope and pockets the other, "Madam, here is a letter from my lord."

Imogen says, "Who, your lord? That is my lord Leonatus? Oh, smart indeed would be that astrologer that knew the stars as I do his writing. He would lay the future open."

She turns to the shrine and presents the letter, "You good gods, let what is contained here relish of love, of my lord's health, of his happiness, but not that we two are apart; let that grieve him: some griefs are curable; that is one of them, for it invigorates love: of his happiness, all but in that."

She turns away from the shrine and breaks the envelope's seal, "Good wax, your leave. Blessed be you bees that make these locks of counsel. You clasp Cupid's letters."

She reads the letter and exclaims, "Good news, gods."

She reads aloud, "'Justice, and your father's wrath, should he find me in his kingdom, could not be so cruel to me, if you, oh the dearest of creatures, would renew me with your eyes. I am in Cambria, at Milford-Haven: what your own love advises you from this news, follow. Wishing you all happiness, that remains loyal to my vow, and yours, increasing in love, Leonatus Posthumus.'"

She says, "Oh, for a horse with wings: Did you hear that, Pisanio? He is at Milford-Haven: read, and tell me how far it is from here. If one of ordinary affairs may plod it in a week, why can't I glide there in a day? Then, true Pisanio, who longs like me, to see your lord; who longs–let me flutter–but not like me: yet longs, but in a fainter kind. Oh, not like me: for mine is beyond beyond: say, and speak in details–love's counsellor should fill the ears to the smothering of the sense–how far it is to this blessed Milford: and tell me how Wales was made so happy as to inherit such a haven: but first, how can we sneak out of here, and excuse the gap that we shall make in time from our leaving to our return: but first, how do we get there quickly?"

She stops and calms herself, "Why worry about excuses now? We will talk of that after. Please, speak, how many score of miles may we well ride between hour and hour?"

Pisanio says, "One score between sun and sun, madam, is enough for you." He thinks, "and too much too."

56.

Imogen says, "Why, one riding to his execution could never go so slow. I have heard of riding wagers, where horses have been faster than the sands of time. But this is foolery: go ask my woman to pretend a sickness; say she'll go home to her father: and provide me a riding-suit, no more costly than would be appropriate to a free-holder's housewife."

Pisanio says, "Madam, you best consider."

Imogen gestures with her hands, "I see what is before me, man: not here, nor there, nor what will happen, they have a fog that I cannot look through. Away. Do as I asked: there's nothing more to say, our target is Milford."

III-3

Wales. A rock cave in the mountains near Milford-Haven.

Two strapping young men in their early twenties, Arviragus, known as Cadwell, and Guiderius, known as Polydore, appear at the cave opening.

An older man, Belarius, known as Morgan, is in front stopped at the opening, "A good day not to stay inside with roofs as low as ours:"

He goes to his knees at the entrance and so do the young men.

Belarius says, "Stoop, boys; this gate teaches you how to adore the heavens and bows you to a morning's holy prayers: the gates of kings are so high that giants may strut through and keep their imperial turbans on, without greeting the sun."

He steps outside, "Hail, you fair heaven! We live in the rock, so don't use you as much as prouder livers do."

Guiderius steps outside, "Hail, heaven!"

Arviragus steps outside, "Hail, heaven!"

They are dressed in clothes of skins, cut nobly yet still primitive.

Belarius says, "Now for our mountain sport: up to yonder hill; your legs are young; I'll walk these flats. Consider, when you are on high and see me as small as a crow, that it is place which diminishes and sets off; and you may then think of the tales I've told you of courts, of princes, of the tricks in war: where service is not service, just being done, but on being accepted: to understand that, draws profit from everything we see; and often, to our comfort, we shall find the sharded beetle in a safer home than the full-winged eagle. Oh, this life is nobler than serving for criticisms, richer than doing nothings for a badge, prouder than the rustle of unpaid-for silk: such gain the generosity of a fine tailor yet never pay the account: no life compared to ours."

Guiderius says, "You speak out of your own experience: we, poor unfledged, have never flown from sight of the nest, nor know what the air is like away from home. It happens that this life is good, if a quiet life is good; sweeter to you that have a painful knowledge; corresponding well with your stiff age: but to us it is a cell of ignorance; traveling only in our dreams; a prison for a debtor, that doesn't dare over step the limit."

Arviragus says, "What should we talk about when we are as old as you? When we hear the rain and wind beat dark December? How, squeezed in our cave, shall we talk the freezing hours away? We have seen nothing; we are beastlike, stealthy as the fox after prey, as warlike as the wolf for what we eat; our valour is to chase what flees; in our cage we make song together, as do imprisoned birds, and sing our bondage freely."

Belarius says, "How you talk. If you knew the city's moneylenders and felt them knowingly; the art of the court as hard to leave as keep; whose climb to the top is certain falling, or so slippery that the fear is as bad as falling; the toil of war, an endeavor that only seems to seek out danger in the name of fame and honour, to die in the search, and have a slanderous epitaph as often as a record of fair act; constantly ill treated for doing well; what's worse, must remain courteous at the censure. Oh boys, the world may read this story in me: my body is marked with Roman swords, and my word was once first with the best of reputation. Cymbeline loved me, and when a soldier was the topic, my name was not far off: then I was like a tree whose boughs are bent with fruit. But in one night, a storm or robbery, call it what you will, shook down my ripened hangings, indeed, my very leaves, and left me bare to the weather."

Guiderius says, "Uncertain favour."

Belarius says, "My fault was nothing–as I've told you often–but that two villains, whose lies prevailed over my perfect honour, swore to Cymbeline I was an accomplice to the Romans: my banishment followed, and for twenty years this rock and these surroundings have been my world; where I have lived at honest freedom, paid more pious debts to heaven than in all my early years."

He waves his arms changing the subject, "But to the mountains, this is not hunters' talk: he that strikes the game first shall be lord of the feast; the other two shall serve him; and we won't fear poison, which is often found in places of greater state. I'll meet you in the valleys."

Guiderius and Arviragus leave, splitting up.

Belarius walks to the forest edge while the boys run into the hills to circle around and drive the game.

Belarius looks at the ground, "How hard it is to hide the sparks of nature? These boys don't know they are sons to the king; nor does Cymbeline dream they are alive. They think they are mine; and though trained up modestly in the cave where they bow, their thoughts hit the roofs of palaces, and nature prompts them in simple and low things to play the prince much better than others do with trickery. This Polydore, the heir of Cymbeline and Britain, who the king his father called Guiderius. Jupiter, when I sit on my three-legged stool and tell the warlike feats I have done, his spirits fly out into my story: say 'my enemy fell, and I set my foot on his neck;' the princely blood flows in his cheek, he sweats, strains his young nerves and puts himself in postures that act my words. The younger brother, Cadwal, once Arviragus, in the same way strikes life into my speech and shows much more his own roots."

Noises from the forest get his attention, "Hear that, the game is roused.

60.

"Oh Cymbeline, heaven and my conscience knows you banished me unjustly, so I stole these babes; thinking to bar you from succession, as you took my lands. Euriphile was their nurse; they took her for their mother, and every day honour her grave: myself, Belarius, called Morgan, they take for their natural father."

Belarius freezes at a sound from the woods, and whispers, "The game is up."

III-4

A deserted country path in the hills across the Severn.

Pisanio and Imogen are walking. She shows signs of exhaustion and they stop.

Pisanio looks all around to be sure they are alone.

Imogen says, "You told me, when we left the horses, the place was near at hand: my mother didn't take this long to birth me. Pisanio, man: Where is Posthumus?"

She looks at Pisanio and discovers him staring at her.

She asks, "What is in your mind, that makes you stare so? Why does that sigh break from inside you? One, painted like this, would be interpreted as perplexed beyond self-understanding: put yourself into a manner less fearful, before wildness overruns my calmer senses. What's the matter?"

He holds out Posthumus's letter, pocketed earlier.

Imogen asks, "Why tender that paper to me, with a look untender? If it is summer news, smile; if winterly, you need only keep that same look."

She takes the letter, "My husband's hand? That damned Italian has outwitted him, and he's in some trouble. Speak, man: your tongue may take the edge off some extremity, which to read would be mortal to me."

Pisanio says, "Please, read; and you shall find me a wretched man, a thing the most disdained by fortune."

62.

Imogen reads aloud, "'Your mistress, Pisanio, has played the strumpet in my bed; the testimonies lie bleeding in me. I don't speak out of weak assumption, but from proof as strong as my grief and as certain as I expect my revenge. That part you, Pisanio, must act for me, if your faithfulness is not tainted with her breach. Let your own hands take her life: I shall give you opportunity at Milford-Haven. She has my letter for the purpose where, if you fear to strike and to make me certain it is done, you are the pimp to her dishonour and equally disloyal to me.'"

Pisanio watches her, thinking, "Why do I need to draw my sword? the paper has cut her throat already. No, it is slander, whose edge is sharper than the sword, whose tongue outvenoms all the snakes of the Nile, whose breath rides on the speeding winds and lives in all corners of the world: kings, queens and nobles, maids, matrons, no, the secrets of the grave this viperous slander enters."

She drops the letter to her side.

Pisanio says, "Are you well, madam?"

Imogen says, "False to his bed? What is it to be false? To lie awake there and think about him? To weep hour after hour? If sleep does come, to break it with an anxious dream of him and cry myself awake? That's false to his bed, is it?"

Pisanio says, "Alas, good lady."

Imogen says, "I'm false? Your conscience witness: Iachimo, you accused him of infidelity; you looked like a villain then; now I think your favour is good. Some chippie of Italy–painted like her mother–has betrayed him: I am stale, a robe out of fashion; and, since I am too worthy to hang on the wall, I must be ripped: to pieces with me: Oh! Men's vows are women's traitors. All those seeming good–by your revolt, oh husband–shall be thought put on for villainy; not born where it grows, but worn as bait for ladies."

Pisanio says, "Good madam, hear me."

Imogen says, "True honest men being heard, like false Aeneas, were in his time thought false, and Sinon's weeping scandaled many a holy tear, took pity from most true wretchedness: so you, Posthumus, will set the pattern for all men; goodly and gallant shall be false and perjured, from your great failing.

"Come, fellow, be honest: do your master's bidding: when you see him, tell him of my obedience."

She takes Pisanio's sword from its scabbard, "Look, I draw the sword myself, take it, and hit the innocent mansion of my love, my heart; fear not; it's empty of all but grief: your master is not there, who was once the riches of it. Do his bidding; strike, you may be valiant in a better cause; but now you seem a coward."

Pisanio pushes the sword aside, "Go, vile instrument, you shall not damn my hand."

Imogen says, "Why, I must die; and if not by your hand, you are no servant of your master's. There is a divine prohibition against self-slaughter that cowards my weak hand."

She indicates her chest, "Come, here's my heart. Something is in front of it. Wait, wait, we'll put up no defence; obedient as the scabbard. What is here?"

She pulls out the first letter from Posthumus, "The scriptures of the loyal Leonatus, all turned to heresy?"

She throws the letter down, "Away, away, corrupters of my faith, you shall no more be stomach to my heart. That is how poor fools believe false teachers: though those that are betrayed do feel the treason sharply, yet the traitor stands in worse case of woe. And you, Posthumus, you that set up my disobedience against my father the king and made me contemptuous of the suits of princely fellows, shall find it was no act of common occurrence, but a strain of rareness: and I grieve myself to think, when you lose your appetite for her that you now expend yourself on, how your memory will then be panged by me."

She addresses Pisanio, "Pray you, carry out the task. The lamb pleads to the butcher: where's your knife? you are too slow to do your master's bidding, when I desire it too."

Pisanio says, "Oh gracious lady, since I received the order to do this business I have not slept one wink."

Imogen says, "Do it then and go to bed."

Pisanio says, "I'll wake my eye-balls blind first."

Imogen says, "Why did you undertake it then? Why have you wasted so many miles with a pretence? this place? My action and your own? our horses' labour? The perturbed court for my being absent? Where I was never meant to return. Why have you gone so far, to be undone when you have taken your post, the elected game before you?"

Pisanio says, "To win time to lose such bad employment. Time to consider a plan. Good lady, hear me with patience."

Imogen says, "Talk your tongue weary; I have heard I am a strumpet; and my ear having been struck false, can take no greater wound, nor probe to bottom that. But speak."

Pisanio says, "Then, madam, I thought you would not go back again."

Imogen says, "Most like; bringing me here to kill me."

Pisanio says, "Not so: but if I were as wise as honest, then my purpose would prove well. It can only be that my master is deceived: some villain, yes, and top in his art, has done you both this cursed injury."

Imogen says, "Some Roman courtezan."

Pisanio says, "No, on my life.

"I'll send word you are dead and send him some bloody sign. It is commanded I should. You'll be missed at court, and that will confirm it."

Imogen says, "Good fellow, what will I do and where? where will I live and how? What comfort is there in such a life when I am dead to my husband?"

Pisanio says, "If you go back to the court–"

She cuts him off with strength, "No court, no father; no more ado with that harsh, noble ranked, simple nothing, that Cloten, whose love-suit has been as fearful as a siege."

Pisanio says, "If not at court, then you must not stay in Britain."

Imogen says, "Where then? Has Britain all the sun that shines? Day, night, aren't they only in Britain? In the world's volume our Britain seems as of it, but not in it; in a great pool a swan's nest: I ask you, think there are livers out of Britain."

Pisanio smiles at her sarcasm, "I'm glad you think of other places. The ambassador, Lucius the Roman, comes to Milford-Haven tomorrow: now, if you could wear thoughts as dark as your fortune, and disguise that which to be seen would bring self-danger, you can walk in full view; near the residence of Posthumus; so close that though his actions won't be visible, hourly reports would render him to your ear as he moves."

Imogen says, "Oh, for such means, though it imperils my modesty, it isn't death on it, I will risk it."

66.

Pisanio says, "Well, then, here's the point: you must forget to be a princess: change command into obedience: you must forget to be a woman: change fear and coyness–the handmaids of all women, or, more truly, woman its pretty self–into an impish courage: ready to scoff, quick to react, saucy and as quarrelsome as a weasel; you must forget that rarest treasure of your cheek, exposing it–but, oh, the harder heart, alack, no remedy–to the greedy touch of common-kissing sycophants: and forget your elaborate and dainty clothes, which make Jupiter's wife envious."

Imogen says, "Be brief, I see where you're going with this, and am almost a man already."

Pisanio says, "First, make yourself like one. Planning ahead, I have already packed doublet, hat, stockings, all that answer to them: with their help, and with what imitation you can borrow from youth of that age, present yourself before noble Lucius, desire his service, tell him your accomplishments–which you'll make him understand, if he has an ear for music–doubtless he will embrace you with joy, for he is honourable and more than that, most holy. For your means abroad, you have me, and I will never fail."

Imogen says, "You are the only comfort the gods chose for me. Please, let's go: there's more to be considered; but we'll do all that time will allow: I am up to this attempt, and will do it with a prince's courage. Let's go, I ask you."

Pisanio says, "Well, madam, we must take a short farewell, in case, being missed, I am suspected of taking you from the court."

Imogen pauses to consider that she must now go on alone.

She looks to her destination in the distance.

Pisanio offers the little box with the lily on top, "My noble mistress, here is a box the queen gave me. What's in it is precious; if you are sick at sea, or have an upset stomach on land, a portion of this will drive away the illness.

"To some cover, and put on your man clothes. May the gods direct you to the best."

Imogen says, "Amen: I thank you."

III-5

The court hall in Cymbeline's palace.

King Cymbeline, the Queen, Cloten, the Lords, and all Attendants enter and settle.

The Queen takes her place on one side of the King and Cloten automatically sits in the other.

Cymbeline gestures and Caius Lucius is shown in.

Cymbeline says, "So far; and so fare you well."

Caius Lucius says, "Thanks, royal sir. My emperor has written, I must leave quickly; and am very sorry to report you are my master's enemy."

Cymbeline says, "Our subjects, sir, will not endure his yoke; and for ourself to show less sovereignty than they, would appear unkinglike."

Caius Lucius says, "So, sir: I desire from you a safe conduct overland to Milford-Haven. Madam, all joy befall your grace, and you."

Cymbeline indicates the First and Second Lords, "My lords, you are appointed for that duty. In no point omit the due of honour. So farewell, noble Lucius."

Caius Lucius turns to Cloten and offers his hand, "Your hand, my lord."

They shake.

Cloten says, "Receive it friendly; but from this time on I wear it as your enemy."

Caius Lucius says, "Sir, the event is yet to name the winner: fare you well."

Cymbeline instructs the Lords, "Do not leave the worthy Lucius, until he has crossed the Severn. Happiness."

Caius Lucius and the Lords go out.

The Queen says, "He leaves frowning: but it honours us that we have given him cause."

Cloten says, "It is all the better; your valiant Britons have their wishes in it."

Cymbeline says, "Lucius already wrote to the emperor how it goes here. We should make our chariots and horsemen ready promptly: the forces he already has in France will soon be drawn together, he will move his war against Britain from there."

The Queen says, "It is not sleepy business; but must be looked to speedily and strongly."

Cymbeline says, "Our expectation that it would be so has made us ready."

He looks at Cloten in Imogen's seat, "But, my gentle queen, where is our daughter? She has not appeared before the Roman, nor to fulfill the duty of the day to us. She looks at us like a thing made more of malice than of duty: we have noticed."

He speaks to an Attendant, "Call her before us," and the Attendant leaves on the errand.

Cymbeline says, "We have been too tolerant."

70.

The Queen says, "Royal sir, since the exile of Posthumus, her life has been most retired; the cure, my lord, will take time. Please your majesty, refrain from sharp talk: she's a lady so sensitive of criticism that words are lashes and lashes death to her."

The Attendant reappears shaking his head.

Cymbeline says, "Where is she, sir? How can her contempt be answered?"

The Attendant says, "Please you, sir, her chambers are all locked; and there's no answer given to the loudest noise we can make."

The Queen says, "My lord, when I last went to visit her, she asked me to make her excuses for keeping to her room constrained by her infirmity, she could not do her duty, which she was bound to pay you daily: She wished me to make it known; but our special court made me forget."

Cymbeline says, "Her doors locked? Not seen of late? I hope to heaven that what I fear proves false." He storms out.

The Queen says, "Son, follow the king."

Cloten says, "That man of hers, Pisanio, has not been seen for two days."

The Queen says, "Go, look after."

Cloten goes out.

The Queen smiles greedily, "Pisanio, that stand so for Posthumus.

"He has a drug of mine; I hope his absence continues by swallowing it, for he believes it is a thing most precious.

"What about her, where is she gone? With any luck, despair has seized her, or, with wings of love, she's flown to her desired Posthumus and gone to her death or dishonour. I can make good use of either: she being down, I have the placing of the British crown."

Cloten comes back in, in a rush.

The Queen asks, "What news, my son?"

Cloten says, "It is certain she has fled. Go in and cheer the king: he rages; none dare approach him."

The Queen thinks, "All the better: may this night prevent him from seeing the coming day." She goes in.

Cloten says, "I love and hate her: for she's fair and royal, and that she has all courtly parts more exquisite than any lady, all ladies, all womankind; from every one take the best compounded into one and she excels them all. Therefore I love her. But dissing me and throwing her favours on the low Posthumus slanders her judgment that what is else rare is choked; and I will conclude to hate her, no, indeed, to be revenged upon her. For when fools shall–"

Pisanio is heading out the door carrying a bag when Cloten spots him, "Who is here? Are you packing, peasant? Come here."

He recognizes Pisanio, "Ah, you precious pimp, villain, where is your lady?"

He pulls a dagger, "In a word; or else you join the fiends of hell."

Pisanio says, "Oh, good my lord."

Cloten says, "Where is your lady? Or, by Jupiter, I will not ask again. Quickly villain, I'll have this secret from your heart, or rip your heart to find it. Is she with Posthumus? From whose many weights of commonness cannot draw a dram of worth."

72.

Pisanio says, "How can she be with him? When was she missed? He is in Rome."

Cloten says, "Where is she, sir? Come nearer; no more stalling: satisfy me thoroughly what is become of her."

Pisanio says, "Oh, my all-worthy lord."

Cloten's dagger punctures Pisanio's skin and draws blood, "All-worthy villain, disclose where your mistress is at once, at the next word: no more of 'worthy lord': Speak, or your silence is your condemnation and your death."

Pisanio presents the letter Imogen discarded, "Then, sir, this is the history of my knowledge about her flight."

Cloten grabs it, "Let's see it. I will pursue her even to Augustus' throne."

Pisanio takes out a handkerchief to wipe the blood, thinking, "This, or perish. She's far enough; and what he learns by this may prove his travel, not her danger."

Cloten says, "Hum," still reading.

Pisanio thinks, "I'll write to my lord she's dead. Oh Imogen, safe may you wander, safe return again."

Cloten finishes reading and says, "Peasant, is this letter true?"

Pisanio says, "Sir, as far as I know."

Cloten says, "It is Posthumus' hand; I know it. Peasant, if you would not be a villain, but do me true service, undergo those employments wherein I should have cause to use you with a serious industry, that is, whatever villainy I ask you do, to perform it directly and truly, I would think you an honest man: you would neither want my means for your relief nor my voice for your advancement."

Pisanio says, "Well, my good lord."

Cloten pulls out his coin purse and takes out several gold pieces, "Will you serve me? for since patiently and constantly you have stuck to the bare fortune of that beggar Posthumus, you can not, from simple gratitude be anything but a faithful follower of mine: will you serve me?"

Pisanio says, "Sir, I will."

Cloten says, "Give me your hand; here's my pay. Have you any of your master's garments in your possession?"

Pisanio says, "I have, my lord, at my lodging, the same suit he wore when he took leave of my lady and mistress."

Cloten says, "The first service you do me, fetch that suit here: let it be your first service; go."

Pisanio says, "I shall, my lord."

Pisanio goes out to get the clothes, which he retrieves from the dirty laundry nearby and overhears Cloten, "Meet you at Milford-Haven–I forgot to ask him something; I'll remember it eventually–you villain Posthumus, I will kill you right there. I wish these clothes were here. She said once–the bitterness of it I now expel from my heart–that she held the very garment of Posthumus in more respect than my noble and natural person together with the adornment of my qualities. With that suit upon my back, I will ravish her: first kill him in front of her; she will see my valour, she will regret her contempt. He on the ground, my last insults spoken over his dead body, and when my lust has

74.

feasted–which, as I say, to spite her I will do in the clothes she praised–I'll knock her back to the court, walk her home again. She has despised me happily, and I'll be merry in my revenge."

Pisanio makes a loud entrance with the clothes. Cloten clutches at them and fingers them, "Are these the garments?"

Pisanio says, "Yes, my noble lord."

Cloten says, "How long since she went to Milford-Haven?"

Pisanio says, "She can barely be there yet."

Cloten says, "Bring these clothes to my room; that is the second thing I command you: the third is, that you will be a voluntary mute to my plan. Be but duteous, and true advancement shall come your way. My revenge is now at Milford: I wish I had wings to follow it. Come, and be true."

Cloten leaves.

Pisanio says, "You send me to lose: being true to you would prove false, which I will never be, to him that is most true. Go to Milford, and don't find her. Flow heavenly blessings upon her: Stifle this fool's speed with slowness; let the effort be his only reward."

III-6

Wales. Before the mountain cave.

Imogen, in a page's clothes, plods along a narrow road, "I see a man's life is a tedious one: I have tired myself, and two nights in a row made the ground my bed. I should be sick, but my resolve restores me. Milford, when Pisanio showed you to me from the mountain-top you were within sight."

She stumbles weakly, "Oh Jupiter, I think charities reject the wretched; such, I mean, where they should be relieved. Two beggars told me I could not miss my way: will poor folks lie, that have afflictions on them, knowing it is a punishment or trial? Yes; no wonder, when rich ones scarcely tell the truth. To lapse in fulness is worse than to lie for need, and falsehood is worse in kings than beggars. My dear lord, you are one of the false ones. Now I think on you, my hunger's gone; but just before that, I was at the point of sinking for want of food."

She notices the cave entrance, "But what is this? Here is a path to it: it is some savage's home: best not to call; I dare not call: yet famine, before it overthrows nature, makes one brave; plenty and peace breeds cowards: hardship is mother of hardiness."

She calls out, "Hello? Who's here? If any thing that's civilized, speak; if savage, take or lend. Hello?

"No answer? Then I'll enter."

She stops herself, "Best draw my sword: and hope my enemy fears the sword like me, he'll scarcely look on it."

She draws her sword, "Such a foe, good heavens."

She moves inside the cave.

III-7

Belarius, Guiderius, and Arviragus appear out of the forest carrying the dead game.

Belarius says, "You, Polydore, have proved best hunter and are master of the feast: Cadwal and I will play the cook and servant; it is our agreement: the sweat of industry would dry and die, but for the end it works to. Come; our stomachs will make what is plain savoury: weariness can snore on flint, when lazy sloth finds the down pillow hard. Now peace be here, poor house, that keeps yourself."

Guiderius says, "I am thoroughly weary."

Arviragus says, "I am weak with toil, yet strong in appetite."

Guiderius says, "There is cold meat in the cave; we'll eat that, while what we have killed is cooked."

Belarius starts into the cave and backs out, "Stay; don't come in. Except that it's eating our food, I thought there was a fairy here."

Guiderius says, "What's the matter, sir?"

Belarius says, "By Jupiter, an angel: or an earthly match. Look at divineness no older than a boy."

Imogen comes out of the cave, startled. She eyes her sword left against the wall and sees Guiderius and Arviragus assume defensive stances.

She takes a step away from her weapon, "Good masters, do me no harm: before I entered, I called out; and meant to have begged or bought what I took: I pledge this is true, I have stolen nothing, nor would I, even though I found gold strewn on the floor."

She reaches for the silver coins she had been about to set down, "Here's money for my meat: I would have left it on the board as soon as I had finished eating, and left saying prayers for the provider."

Guiderius says, "Money, youth?"

Arviragus says, "All gold and silver should turn to dirt. It is only valued by those who worship dirty gods."

Imogen says, "I see you're angry: I wish you to know, if you kill me for my fault, I would have died had I not made it."

Belarius says, "Where are you bound?"

Imogen says, "To Milford-Haven."

Belarius says, "What's your name?"

Imogen says, "Fidele, sir. I have a kinsman who is bound for Italy; he embarked at Milford; it was to him I was going, weak with hunger, when I fell in this offence."

Belarius breaks into a wide grin, "Please you, fair youth, don't think we are peasants. Don't measure our good minds by this crude place we live in. Well met, it is almost night: you shall have better cheer before you depart: and thanks to stay and eat it. Boys, bid him welcome."

Imogen is bewildered.

Guiderius says, "If you were a woman, youth, I should woo hard to be your groom. In honesty, I bid for you as I would buy."

Arviragus says, "I'll accept he is a man; I'll love him as my brother: And such a welcome as I would give him after a long absence is yours. Most welcome; be in good spirits, for you fall amongst friends."

78.

Imogen thinks, "Amongst friends? If brothers: If only they had been my father's sons, then my value would have been less, and so more equal to you, Posthumus."

Belarius says, "He worries with some distress."

Guiderius says, "I wish I could relieve it."

Arviragus says, "Or I, whatever it is, whatever the pain it cost, whatever the danger: God's!"

Belarius says, "Listen, boys." They huddle and whisper together.

Imogen thinks, "Great men, that had a court no bigger than this cave, that attended themselves and had the virtue which their own conscience sealed in them–setting aside that nothing-gift of differing multitudes–could not surpass these two.

"Pardon me, gods, I wish to change into a man to be companion with them, since Leonatus is false."

Belarius breaks the huddle, "It shall be so. Boys, we'll go dress our game.

"Young man, come in. Talk is heavy work on an empty stomach. When we have eaten, we'll ask for your story, as much as you will tell us."

Guiderius says, "Please, draw near."

Arviragus says, "Not the night to the owl nor the morning to the lark is less welcome."

Imogen says, "Thanks, sir."

Arviragus says, "Please, draw near."

III-7

Rome. A public place.

Two Senators enter and approach a gathering of Tribunes.

The First Senator says, "This is the substance of the Emperor's decree: that since the common forces are now in action against the Pannonians and Dalmatians, and that the legions now in France are too weak to undertake our war against the rebel Britons, that we call upon the gentry to take care of this. He makes Lucius preconsul: and to you the Tribunes, for this immediate levy, he commands his absolute commission. Long live Caesar."

The First Tribune asks, "Is Lucius general of the forces?"

The Second Senator says, "Yes."

The First Tribune says, "Remaining now in France?"

The First Senator says, "With those legions I spoke of, where you are to send your supplies and forces: the words of your commission will give the numbers and time of their dispatch."

The First Tribune says, "We will discharge our duty."

IV-1

Wales. Before the mountain cave.

Cloten appears from the trees in the clothes Posthumus wore at the palace. They fit quite well. He puts his own clothes in his saddle bag and looks around, "I am near the place where they were to meet, if Pisanio described it truly."

He lifts his arms and stretches to test the clothes, "How fit his garments serve me? Why should his mistress, who was made by the same god who made the tailor, not fit too? The rather–begging pardon of the word–for it is said a woman's fitness comes by fits: that is why I must play the workman, I dare speak it to myself, for it is not vain-glory for a man and his mirror to confer in his own chamber; I mean, the lines of my body are as well drawn as his; no less young, more strong, not beneath him in fortunes, beyond him in the advantage of the time, above him in birth, alike conversant in general services, and more remarkable in hand to hand combat: yet this imperceptive thing loves him despite me. What a thing mortality is?"

He plucks at the clothes, "Posthumus, your head–which now is growing upon your shoulders–shall be off within this hour; your mistress ravished; your garments cut to pieces before your face: and I'll drive her home to her father; who may be a little angry for my rough usage; but my mother, having power over his testiness, shall twist all into commendations.

"My horse is tied up safe: out, sword, and to a sore purpose: Fortune, put them into my hand: this is the very description of their meeting-place; and the fellow dares not deceive me."

IV-2

The cave entrance.

Belarius, Guiderius, Arviragus, and Imogen come out of the cave.

Imogen, pale and sickly, stumbles and leans heavily on the wall.

Belarius says, "You are not well: remain in the cave; we'll come to you after hunting."

Arviragus addresses Imogen, "Brother, stay here: are we not brothers?"

Imogen says, "So should man and man be; but clay and clay differs in rank, whose dust is both alike. I am very sick."

Guiderius puts his hunting gear down and moves to Imogen's side saying to the others, "Go hunting; I'll stay with him."

Imogen waves him away, "I am not that sick, yet I am not well; but not such a city-bred weakling as to seem to die before being sick: so please, leave me; stick to your plans: the breach of custom is breach of all. I am ill, but your being by me cannot cure me; society is no comfort to one not sociable: I am not very sick, since I can reason it. Pray, trust me: I'll rob none but myself; and let me die, stealing so poorly."

Guiderius says, "I love you; I have spoke it how much the quantity, the weight as much, as I do love my father."

He grabs his hunting gear and rushes away.

Belarius says, "What? How now?"

Arviragus says, "If it is sinful to say so, I join in my good brother's fault: I don't know why I love this youth; and I have heard you say, love's reason is without reason: If Death came to the door and asked who shall die, I would say 'My father, not this youth.'"

Belarius thinks, "Oh noble heredity! Oh natural worthiness! breed of greatness! Cowards father cowards and base things sire base: nature has meal and bran, contempt and grace. I'm not their father; yet whoever this is, accomplishes a miracle itself, being loved before me."

Belarius spurs Arviragus on, "It is the ninth hour of the morn."

Arviragus says, "Brother, farewell."

Imogen says, "I wish you sport."

Arviragus says, "And you health."

Imogen says, "So please you, sir."

She thinks, "These are kind creatures. Gods, what lies I have heard: Our courtiers say everything is savage except at court: experience disproves the report. The imperial seas breed monsters. Poor tributary rivers grow sweet fish for the dish.

"I am sick still; heart-sick. Pisanio, I'll now taste of your drug."

She swallows the medicine from the box with the lily on top.

Arviragus and Belarius join Guiderius who says, "I could not stir him: he said he was fine, but not well; dishonestly afflicted, but yet honest."

Arviragus says, "The same as he answered me, and then said I might learn more later."

Belarius calls to Imogen, "To the field, to the field: We'll leave you for this time: go in and rest."

Arviragus says, "We'll not be away long."

Belarius says, "Please don't be sick, for you must be our housewife."

Imogen says, "Well or ill, I am bound to you. And shall be forever."

Imogen re-enters the cave

Belarius says, "This youth, however distressed, it appears he has had good ancestors."

Arviragus says, "How angel-like he sings?"

Guiderius says, "But his neat cookery? He cut our roots into shapes, and made sauce of our broths, as if Jupiter's wife was sick and he her dietician."

Arviragus says, "Nobly he puts a smile with a sigh, as if the sigh was part of it, for not being such a smile; the smile mocking the sigh, that it would fly from so divine a temple, to mix with winds that sailors curse at."

Guiderius says, "I noticed that grief and patience both, are rooted in him, entangling their spurs."

Arviragus says, "Grow, patience, and make the stinking elder, grief, disentangle his dying root with each increase of the vine."

Belarius says, "It is late morning. Come, away."

They walk on until Belarius notices something and halts them, "Who's there?"

They take cover.

Cloten appears, "I cannot find those traitors; that villain has mocked me. I am tired."

Belarius says, "'Those traitors?' Does he mean us? I think I know him: it is Cloten, the son of the queen."

He panics, "It's an ambush. I haven't seen him in many years, but I know it's him. We are considered as outlaws: run."

Guiderius grabs his arm to calm him, "He is just one: you and my brother search what companies are near. Away. Leave me alone with him."

Arviragus grabs Belarius and they run off to check the surroundings.

Cloten sees them leaving and yells after them, "Wait a moment. Who are you that run away? some villain bandits? I have heard of such."

He sees Guiderius appear beside him and tenses, "What slave are you?"

Guiderius replies, "I never did a thing more slavish than to answer to the name slave without a fight."

Cloten says, "You are a robber, a law-breaker, a villain: yield, thief."

Guiderius says, "To who? to you? What are you? Don't I have an arm as big as yours? a heart as big? Your words, granted, are bigger, but I don't wear my dagger in my mouth. Say what you are, why I should yield to you?"

Cloten says, "You simple villain, don't you know me by my clothes?"

Guiderius says, "No, nor your tailor, rascal, your grandfather made those clothes, which, it seems, make you."

Cloten remembers he is not wearing his own clothes, "You precious rogue, my tailor did not make them."

Guiderius laughs and says, "Go, then, and thank the man that gave them to you. You are some fool; I am reluctant to beat you."

Cloten overreacts to the word, "You insolent thief, hear my name, and tremble."

Guiderius says, "What's your name?"

Cloten says, "Cloten, you villain."

Guiderius says, "Cloten, you double villain, be your name, I'm not trembling at it: if it were Toad, or Adder, Spider, it would affect me more."

Cloten says, "To further your fear, no, to your absolute confusion, know I am son to the queen."

Guiderius says, "I am sorry for it; not seeming so worthy as your birth."

Cloten says, "Are you not afraid?"

Guiderius says, "I fear those I revere, the wise: I laugh at fools, not fear them."

Cloten overreacts to the word, "I sentence you to die! When I have slain you with my own hand, I'll follow those that ran away and set your heads on the gates of London-town: yield, country bandit."

They fight and move deeper into the woods.

Belarius and Arviragus return from different directions and meet up.

Belarius says, "No companies abroad?"

Arviragus says, "None in the world: you must have made a mistake."

Belarius says, "I can't tell: It is long since I saw him, but time has not blurred those sturdy looks which he wore then; the snatches in his voice, and burst of speaking, were his: I am positive it was Cloten."

Arviragus says, "This is where we left them: I hope my brother makes good time with him, you say he is so fierce."

Belarius says, "Having scarcely reached manhood he has no understanding of roaring terrors. Mistakes in judgment often cause fear."

He sees Guiderius returning, "There's your brother."

Guiderius approaches carrying Cloten's severed head by the hair, "This Cloten was a fool, an empty purse," shakes the head, "No money in it: Hercules couldn't knock out his brains, for he had none: yet if I had not done this, the fool would have taken my head as I took his."

Belarius says, "What have you done?"

Guiderius says, "I know precisely what: cut off the head of one Cloten, son to the queen, according to him. He called me traitor, bandit, and swore he would single handedly take us and displace our heads from where–thank the gods–they grow, and set them on London-town."

Belarius says, "We are all undone."

Guiderius says, "Why, worthy father, what have we to lose, but that he swore to take our lives? The law doesn't protect us: then why should we let an arrogant piece of flesh threaten us, play judge and executioner all by himself, because we fear the law? What company did you discover abroad?"

Belarius says, "Not a single soul, but he must have some attendants. Though his bad humour was nothing but mutation, from one bad thing to worse; not frenzy, not absolute madness could have driven him to come here alone; although it may be heard at court that those of us who cave here and hunt here, are outlaws, and might in time make some stronger force. If on hearing this–as is like him–might break out, and swear he would fetch us in; yet it isn't probable to come alone, either by his own undertaking, or theirs: therefore we have good reason to fear that this body has a tail more perilous than the head."

Arviragus says, "Let what is ordained come as the gods predict it. Whatever, my brother has done well."

Belarius despairs, "I was not in the mood to hunt today: Fidele's sickness made my walk from home tedious."

Guiderius says, "With his own sword, which he waved against my throat, I have taken his head from him. I'll throw it into the creek behind our rock; and send it to the sea, and tell the fishes he's the queen's son, Cloten: that's all I care."

He walks away swinging the head.

Belarius says, "I'm afraid it will be revenged: I wish, Polydore, you had not done it: though valour becomes you."

Arviragus says, "I wish I had done it so the revenge would pursue me alone: Polydore, I love you brotherly, but I am jealous you robbed me of this deed: I wish revenges would come for us and put us to the test."

Belarius says, "Well, it is done: we'll hunt no more today, nor seek danger where there's no gain. To our rock; you and Fidele play the cooks: I'll stay until hasty Polydore returns, and bring him to dinner presently."

Arviragus says, "Poor sick Fidele, I'll go to him willingly: to bring back his colour I would bleed a village of such Clotens, and praise myself for charity."

Arviragus leaves.

Belarius looks at the ground, "Oh you goddess, you divine nature, how much of yourself is emblazoned in these two princely boys: they are as gentle as breezes blowing beneath the violet, not wagging his sweet head; and yet as rough, should their royal blood be enraged, as the rudest wind, that takes the mountain pine by the top, and makes him stoop to the valley. It is wonderful that instinct should frame them to royalty unlearned, honour untaught, civility not seen from other, valour that grows wildly in them, but yields a crop as if it had been sowed.

"Still it's a wonder what Cloten's being here means to us, or what his death will bring us."

Guiderius returns, "Where's my brother? I have sent Cloten's thick head down the stream, on a journey to his mother: his body is hostage for his return."

A mournful horn sounds from the cave.

Belarius says, "My ingenious instrument–listen, Polydore–it sounds: but what reason has Cadwal to use it? Listen."

Guiderius says, "Is he at home?"

Belarius says, "He went there just now."

Guiderius says, "What does he mean? It hasn't sounded since the death of our dearest mother. Solemn things should relate to solemn incidents. What is the matter? Triumphs for nothing and lamenting for trifles is jollity for fools and grief for boys. Is Cadwal mad?"

Belarius sees Arviragus approaching, "Look, here he comes, and brings the dire reason in his arms."

Arviragus appears carrying Imogen, as dead, in his arms.

Arviragus says, "The bird is dead that we have made so much on. I'd rather have skipped from sixteen years of age to sixty, to have turned my leaping-time into a crutch, than to have seen this."

Guiderius says, "Oh sweetest, fairest lily: My brother wears you not half so well as when you grew yourself."

Belarius says, "Oh melancholy, who ever yet could sound your bottom? find the ooze, to show what coast your sluggish barge might easily harbour in? You blessed thing, Jupiter knows what man you might have made; but I know you died, a most rare boy, of melancholy. How was he when you found him?"

Arviragus says, "Stark, as you see: smiling like this, as if some fly had tickled slumber, death's dart being laughed at; his right cheek reposing on a cushion."

Guiderius says, "Where?"

Arviragus says, "On the floor; his arms together like this: I thought he slept, and took off my hobnailed boots, whose rudeness made my steps too loud."

Guiderius says, "Why, he is only sleeping: if he is gone, we'll make his grave a bed; his tomb will be haunted with female fairies, and worms will not come to you."

Arviragus says, "As long as summer lasts and I live here, Fidele, I will sweeten your sad grave with the prettiest flowers: you shall not lack the flower that's like your face, pale primrose, nor the azured harebell, like your veins, no, nor the leaf of eglantine, whom not to slander, did not out-sweeten your breath: the robin would, with charitable bill–to shame those rich-left heirs that let their fathers lie without a monument–bring you all this; yes, and furred moss besides, when the flowers are gone, to winter-ground your corpse."

90.

Guiderius says, "Finish; and do not play in womanish words with that which is so serious. Let us bury him, and not lengthen with admiration what is now due debt. To the grave."

Arviragus says, "Where shall we lay him?"

Guiderius says, "By good Euriphile, our mother."

Arviragus says, "Be it so: and, Polydore, though now our voices have the mannish crack, let us sing him to the ground, as we did our mother; use the same notes and words, except that Euriphile must be Fidele."

Guiderius says, "Cadwal, I can't sing: I'll weep, and say the words with you; because notes of sorrow out of tune are worse than priests and soothsayers that lie."

Arviragus says, "We'll speak it, then."

Belarius says, "Great griefs, Cloten is quite forgot. He was a queen's son, boys; and though he came to be our enemy, remember that was his duty: though ordinary and mighty, rotting together, become the same dust, yet reverence, that angel of the world, makes distinction of place between high and low. Our foe was princely and though you took his life, because he was our foe, we must bury him as a prince."

Guiderius says, "Bring him here. A foot soldier's body is as good as a general's when neither is alive."

Arviragus says, "If you'll go fetch him, we'll say our song while you do. Brother, begin."

Belarius leaves.

Guiderius says, "Wait, we must lay his head to the east; our father has a reason for it."

Arviragus says, "It is true."

Guiderius says, "Come on then, and remove him."

Arviragus reluctantly stoops and adjusts the body, "So."

He rises and stands beside Guiderius, "Begin."

Guiderius recites,
"Fear no more the heat of the sun,
Nor the furious winter's rages;
You your worldly task have done,
Home are gone, and taken your wages:
Golden lads and girls all must,
As chimney-sweepers, come to dust."

Arviragus recites,
"Fear no more the frown of the great;
You are past the tyrant's stroke;
Care no more to clothe and eat;
To you the reed is as the oak:
The sceptre, learning, physic, must
All follow this, and come to dust."

Guiderius recites,
"Fear no more the lightning flash,"

Arviragus recites,
"Nor the all-dreaded thunder-stone;"

Guiderius recites,
"Fear not slander, censure rash;"

Arviragus recites,
"You have finished joy and moan:"

Guiderius and Arviragus recite together,
"All lovers young, all lovers must
Consign to you, and come to dust."

92.

Guiderius recites,
"No exorciser harm you,"

Arviragus recites,
"Nor no witchcraft charm you."

Guiderius recites,
"Ghost unlaid forbear you."

Arviragus recites,
"Nothing ill come near you."

Guiderius and Arviragus recite together,
"Quiet consummation have;
And renowned be your grave."

Belarius returns carrying Cloten's body.

Guiderius says, "We have done our funeral rites: come, lay him down."

Belarius does so and presents a handful of flowers, "Here's a few flowers; but about midnight, I'll bring more: the herbs that have cold dew of the night on them are the best scatterings for graves. You were as flowers, now withered: even as these shall be, which we scatter upon you. Come on, let's go, stay on our knees. The ground that gave them first has them again: their pleasures here are past, so is their pain."

Belarius, Guiderius, and Arviragus knee away and then stand and leave.

*

Imogen stirs and wakes, dreaming, "Yes, sir, to Milford-Haven; which is the way? I thank you: by that bush over there? Please, how far is it? Pittikins: can it be six miles yet? I have gone all night. Faith, I'll lie down and sleep."

She almost settles into sleep again when she startles awake and looks around. She sees the body beside her and immediately turns away from it, "But, wait; no bedfellow? Oh gods and goddesses!"

"These flowers are like the pleasures of the world; this bloody man, the sorrow of it. I hope I'm dreaming; for I thought I was a cave-keeper and cook to honest creatures: but it is not so; it was just a bolt of nothing, shot at nothing, which the brain makes of fumes: our very eyes are sometimes blind like our judgments. Good faith, I tremble still with fear: but if there is left in heaven a drop of pity as small as a wren's eye, feared gods, give me a part of it."

She reluctantly faces the body, "The dream is still here: even when I wake, it is outside me, as it is inside me; not imagined, felt. A headless man? The clothes of Posthumus? I know the shape of his leg: this is his hand; his foot Mercurial; his martial thigh; the muscles of Hercules: but his Jovian face–murder in heaven? How? It is gone. Pisanio, all the curses mad Hecuba gave to the Greeks, and mine as well, be on you: you, conspired with that unreligious demon, Cloten, have here cut off my lord. To write and read will be treacherous from now on. Damned Pisanio with his forged letters has struck the topsail from the bravest vessel of the world!

"Oh Posthumus, alas, where is your head? where is it? Ay me! where is it? Pisanio might have slain you in the heart, and left your head on. How should this be? Pisanio? It is he and Cloten: malice and profit in them have laid this woe here. Oh, all makes sense now, filled with meaning! The drug he gave me, which he said was precious and cordial to me, was murderous to the senses wasn't it? That confirms it: this is Pisanio's deed, and Cloten's"

She dips into the corpse's neck and smears blood on herself, "Oh, give colour to my pale cheek with your blood so that we may seem more horrid to those who chance to find us. Oh, my lord! My lord!"

She falls on the body.

*

At the edge of the clearing Caius Lucius and a Roman Captain appear with other Officers accompanying them. The Soothsayer follows.

The Captain is reporting to Caius Lucius as they scan the surroundings, "In addition, the legions garrisoned in France have crossed the sea, awaiting your orders here at Milford-Haven with your ships: they are in readiness."

Caius Lucius says, "But what news from Rome?"

The Captain says, "The senate has stirred up the inhabitants, and gentlemen of Italy, most willing spirits, promise noble service: and they come under the command of bold Iachimo, Syenna's brother."

Caius Lucius says, "When do you expect them?"

The Captain says, "With the next wind."

Caius Lucius says, "This quick action gives us a fair chance. Command our present armies to be mustered; bid the captains look to it."

He gestures the Soothsayer forward, "Now, sir, what have you dreamed of late of this war's outcome?"

The Soothsayer says, "In the night the gods show me visions–I fast and pray for their intelligence–and so it was I saw Jupiter's bird, the Roman eagle, its wings spread from the spongy south to this part of the west, and there it vanished in the sunbeams: which predicts–unless I misread my own divination–success to the Roman host."

Caius Lucius says, "Dream often so, and never false."

Caius Lucius spots the bodies, "Wait, what trunk is here without his top? The remains speak that at some time it was a worthy building."

He notices Imogen draped across the corpse and is surprised, "How? a page? Dead, or sleeping on him? Must be dead for it's unnatural to sleep on the deceased. Let's see the boy's face."

The Captain turns Imogen and her eyes open.

Captain says, "He's alive, my lord."

Caius Lucius says, "Then he'll tell us about this body. Young one, tell us your story, for it demands investigation. Who is this you make your bloody pillow? Or who was he that defied nature and altered that good picture? What's your interest in this sad wreck? How did it happen? Who is it? What are you?"

Imogen says, "I am nothing: or if not, nothing to be were better. This was my master, a very valiant Briton and a good man, that was slain here by bandits. Alas, there are no more such masters. I could wander from east to west and beg to serve, try many, all good, and serve them truly, and never find another such master."

Caius Lucius says, "Alack, good youth: You move no less with your lamenting than your master in bleeding: say his name, good friend."

96.

Imogen says, "Richard du Champ." She thinks, "If I lie and do no harm by it, though the gods hear, I hope they'll pardon–"

Imogen realizes Caius Lucius has asked a question, "What did you say, sir?"

Caius Lucius says, "Your name?"

Imogen says, "Fidele, sir."

Caius Lucius says, "You prove yourself the very same: your name well fits your faithfulness. Will you take your chance with me? I won't say you will be as well mastered, but, be sure, no less beloved. The Roman emperor's letters, sent by a consul to me, could not recommend you better than your own worth: go with me."

Imogen says, "I'll follow, sir, but first, and if it please the gods, I'll hide my master from the flies."

She starts moving earth with her bare hands, "As deep as these poor pickaxes can dig; and when I have scattered wild wood-leaves and weeds over his grave, and said a century of prayers, such as I can, twice over, I'll weep and sigh; and so leaving his service, follow you, so please, sir, allow me."

Caius Lucius says, "Yes, good youth, and I should be your father rather than your master. My friends, the boy has taught us manly duties: let us find the prettiest plot of daisies we can, and dig a grave with our pikes and partisans: come, grab him by the arm. Boy, he is preferred by you to us, and he shall be interred as soldiers can. Be cheerful; wipe your eyes, some falls are the way to happier rising."

IV-3

A meeting room in Cymbeline's palace.

King Cymbeline stands waiting. Lords and Attendants, including the First Lord, stand behind him.

Pisanio is brought in by an Attendant.

Cymbeline gestures to the Attendant, "Out again and bring me word how it is with her."

The Attendant backs out.

Cymbeline turns to a small shrine, "A fever with the absence of her son, a madness has put her life in danger. Heavens, how deeply you touch me all at once. Imogen, the great part of my comfort, gone. My queen upon a sick bed, and in a time when fearful wars come at me. Her son gone, at the time I need him: it strikes me, past the hope of cure."

He turns from the shrine to Pisanio, "But for you, fellow, who must know about her departure and seems so ignorant, we'll force it from you by a sharp torture."

Pisanio says, "Sir, my life is yours; I humbly set it at your will; but, for my mistress, I know nothing about where she stays, why she's gone, nor when she plans to return. Please your highness, hold me your loyal servant."

The First Lord speaks up, "Pardon my liege, the day that she was missing he was here: I dare be bound he's true and shall perform loyally. As for Cloten, there is nothing not being done to seek him, and he will, no doubt, be found."

Cymbeline says, "The time is troublesome." He dismisses Pisanio, "We'll let it go for now; but our suspicions remain."

A Messenger enters and speaks to the First Lord who addresses the King, "So please your majesty, the Roman legions, from France have landed on your coast, with a supply of Roman gentlemen, sent by the senate."

Cymbeline says, "Now I need the counsel of my son and queen, for I am overwhelmed."

The First Lord says, "My liege, you are prepared to challenge no less than what you hear is coming: come more, you're ready for more: all it needs is to put those powers in motion that want to move."

Cymbeline replies, "I thank you. Let's withdraw; and meet the time as it seeks us. We don't fear what came from Italy to annoy us; but we grieve at bad luck here. Away."

They go out leaving Pisanio alone, "I have had no letter from my master since I wrote him Imogen was slain: it is strange: Nor do I hear from my mistress who promised to send me word often: neither do I know what happened to Cloten; but remain perplexed. The heavens are at work. When I am false I am honest; not true, to be true. These present wars shall find I love my country, even to the note of the king, or I'll fall in them. All other doubts, let them be cleared by time: chance brings in some boats without steering."

IV-4

Wales. The mountain cave entrance.

Belarius, Guiderius, and Arviragus come outside reacting to sounds of troops on the move.

Guiderius says, "The noise is all around us."

Belarius says, "Let's run."

Arviragus says, "What pleasure, sir, can we find in life, to hide from action and adventure?"

Guiderius says, "Besides, what hope do we have in hiding? This way, the Romans must slay us for Britons or receive us for barbarous rebels while they make use of us, and slay us after."

Belarius says, "Sons, we'll go higher into the mountains; dig in there. We can't go to the king's army: newness of Cloten's death–we being not known, not mustered among the bands–may want us to explain where we have lived, and that way discover what we have done, whose sentence would be death drawn on with torture."

Carefully, Guiderius voices his concerns, "This is, sir, a doubt at such a time that doesn't become you, nor satisfy us."

Arviragus says, "It is not likely that when they hear the Roman horses neigh, behold their camp fires, have their eyes and ears so full of urgency as now, that they will waste their time noticing us, to want to know where we came from."

Belarius says, "Oh, I am known by many in the army: years ago at the time Cloten was young, he has not worn from my memory. And, besides, the king has not deserved my service nor your loves; who find in my exile a want of breeding, the certainty of this hard life; ever hopeless to have the courtesies your cradle promised, but to be hot summer's tanlings and the shrinking slaves of winter."

Guiderius says, "Then isn't it better to cease to be. My brother and I are not known to the army; you are so out of thought, and memory is so overgrown, it won't be questioned."

Arviragus says, "By this sun that shines, I'll go there: what a thing it is that I never saw a man die, scarce ever looked on blood, except for cowardly rabbits, hot goats, and venison? Never sat on a horse, except one that had a rider as well as myself, who never wore spurs nor iron on his heel? I am ashamed to look upon the holy sun, to have the benefit of his blessed beams, and yet remain so long a poor unknown."

Guiderius says, "By heavens, I'll go: If you will bless me, sir, and give me leave, I'll take the better care, but if you will not, the peril therefore due will fall on me at the hands of Romans."

Arviragus says, "So say I, amen."

Belarius says, "Since you set so slight a valuation on your lives, I have no reason to reserve my cracked one to more care. I'm with you, boys; if in your country wars you happen to die, that is my bed too, lads: lead, lead."

He thinks, "The time seems long; their blood thinks scorn, until it roars up to show they are born princes."

V-1

On the outskirts of the Roman camp.

Posthumus dressed like a Roman finds a spot to be alone. He pulls out the letter from Pisanio which contains his blood-stained handkerchief.

Posthumus says, "Yes, bloody cloth, I'll keep you, for I wanted you coloured so. You married ones, if each of you takes this course, how many must murder wives much better than themselves for straying just a little?"

He stares at the handkerchief, "Oh Pisanio, every good servant does not carry out all commands: obligated to do only the just ones.

"Gods, if you wanted to avenge my faults, I'd rather not have lived for this: if you had saved the noble Imogen to repent, and struck me instead, a wretch more worthy of your vengeance. But, sadly, you snatch some away for little faults; that's love, to have them fall no more: you permit some second ills with ills, each one worse, and make them repent it, to the doers' gain. But Imogen is your own: do your best wills, and make me blessed to obey. I am brought here among the Italian gentry, and to fight against my lady's kingdom. It is enough that, Britain, I have killed your mistress. Peace. I'll give no wound to you.

"Therefore, good heavens, hear my purpose patiently: I'll take off these Italian weeds and dress the same as a British peasant: and so I'll fight against the army I came with: and so I'll die for you, oh Imogen, even for whom my life is every breath a death; and disguised, unknown, neither pitied nor hated, I'll dedicate myself to the face of peril. Let me make men know more valour in me than my garments show. Gods, put the strength of the Leonati in me: To shame the guise of the world, I will begin the fashion, less without and more within."

102.

He removes his Roman garb and stashes it. Bare chested, he wraps a sash around his head to hold his hair, and loops it twice more around his forehead and nose to serve as a mask.

He rushes into the battle, sword flying.

V-2

In the field of battle the British and Roman forces clash.

The Roman army pushes the British back.

Posthumus spots Iachimo and fights his way toward him.

He picks Iachimo out for a skirmish. Iachimo, in full battle armour, doesn't recognize his bare chested opponent.

Their fighting is furious showing that Iachimo is a skilled warrior but Posthumus is more forceful and disarms him.

At a swordpoint breath from the kill, Posthumus withdraws and leaves Iachimo bleeding but alive.

Iachimo lays on the ground, limp, "The heaviness and guilt within my heart take my manhood away: I have lied about a lady, the princess of this country, and even the air weakens me in revenge; or how else could this rustic soldier, a very peasant, have subdued me in my profession? The knighthoods and honours I wear are titles of scorn. If Britain's gentry are better than this peasant as much as he is better than our lords, the odds are that we are scarcely men and you are gods."

*

King Cymbeline's guards are overwhelmed and he is captured by Roman soldiers.

Belarius, Guiderius, and Arviragus launch a counter attack and rescue Cymbeline and take him from the battlefield.

*

British soldiers start to run away in panic thinking all is lost.

Belarius calls to those fleeing, "Stand, stand, we have the advantage of the ground; the lane is guarded: nothing can defeat us but our fears."

Guiderius and Arviragus both call out, "Stand, stand, and fight."

Posthumus joins their call.

*

On the Roman side, Iachimo staggers back to join Caius Lucius and Imogen.

Caius Lucius reacts badly to his sudden appearance and nearly punctures Iachimo with a sword. He lets Iachimo loose and turns to Imogen, "Away, boy, from the troops, and save yourself; for friends kill friends, and the disorder is such as war were blindfolded."

Iachimo says, "It is their fresh supplies."

Caius Lucius says, "It is a day turned strangely: we reinforce quickly, or flee."

V-3

The outskirts of the battlefield.

Posthumus, his hair loose and sashless, wearing a vest meets a British Lord walking alone, without seconds or other attendants.

The British Lord says, "Did you come from where they made the stand?"

Posthumus says, "I did. Though you, it seems, come from the runaways."

The British Lord says, "I did."

Posthumus says, "No blame to you, sir; for all was lost, except the heavens fought: the king himself without his wings, the army broken, and only the backs of Britons seen, all running through a straight lane; the enemy full-hearted, their tongues lolling with slaughter, having work more plentiful than they have tools to do it, struck some down mortally, some slightly touched, some fell merely through fear; so that the straight pass was plugged with dead men hurt behind, and cowards living to die with lifelong shame."

The British Lord says, "Where was this lane?"

Posthumus says, "Close by the battle, ditched, and walled with turf; which gave advantage to an old soldier, an honourable one, I'm sure; who had as long a breeding as his white beard grew, in doing this for his country: across the lane, he, with two young striplings–lads more likely to run the country fair than to commit such slaughter–fortified the passage; cried to those that fled, 'Our Britain's game die fleeing, not our men: to hell fleet souls that fly backwards. Stand; or we will be the Romans and give you that death like beasts which you shun beastly. You save yourselves only by looking back with a bold defiance: stand, stand.'

106.

"These three, with the confidence of three thousand–for three performers are the show when all the rest do nothing–with this word 'Stand, stand,' accommodated by the place, more persuasive with their own nobleness, which could have turned a stick into a lance, bolstered pale looks, part shame, part spirit renewed; so that some, turned coward only by example–oh, a sin in war, damned in the first beginners–began to grin like lions upon the pikes of the hunters.

"Then began a stop to the chaser, then a retreat, and soon a rout, confusion thick; they ran like chickens, the way they had swooped like eagles; retracing as slaves the strides they had made as victors: and then our cowards, like food fragments on hard voyages, became the life of the need: having found the backdoor open of the unguarded hearts, heavens, how they wound, some already slain; some dying; some of their friends run over in the first wave: ten, chased by one, are now each one the slaughter-man of twenty: those that die or resist are grown the mortal bugs of the field."

The British Lord says, "This was strange luck a narrow lane, an old man, and two boys."

Posthumus says, "Don't wonder about it: you are made rather to wonder at the things you hear than to do any work. Why don't you make up a song about it and sing it as a mockery? Here is one:

"'Two boys, an old man twice a boy, a lane,
Preserved the Britons, was the Romans' bane.'"

The British Lord says, "Don't be angry, sir."

Posthumus says, "Sadly, to what end? Who dares not stand against his foe, I'll be his friend; for if he'll do as he would naturally do, I know he'll quickly run away from my friendship too. You have put me into rhyme."

The British Lord says, "Farewell; you're angry."

Posthumus says, "Still running away?"

The British Lord leaves.

Posthumus says, "This is a lord: Oh miserable nobility, to be in the field, and have to ask 'what news?' of me: Today how many would have given up their honours to have saved their own carcasses? Ran away to do it, and yet died anyway. Whereas I, in my own woe, am charmed, I could not find Death where I heard him groan, nor feel him where he struck: being an ugly monster, it is strange he can hide in fresh cups, soft beds, sweet words; or has more agents than we that draw his knives in war. Well, I will find him for now favouring the Briton, no more a Briton, I resume the part I came in: I will fight no more, but yield to the lowest peasant that touches my shoulder. There is great slaughter made by the Roman; great the punishment the Britons must take. For me, my ransom is death; I came to breathe my last on either side; to end it by some means for Imogen."

Posthumus returns to his stashed clothes and changes back into his Roman gear.

*

Two British Captains and Soldiers approach.

The First Captain says, "Jupiter be praised, Lucius is taken. It is thought the old man and his sons were angels."

The Second Captain says, "There was a fourth man, in simple clothes, that faced the enemy with them."

The First Captain says, "So it is reported: but none of them can be found."

He sees Posthumus, "Hold! Who is there?"

108.

Posthumus replies, "A Roman, who would not be drooping here, if his seconds had answered him."

The Second Captain orders his soldiers, "Lay hands on him; a dog, a leg of Rome shall not return to tell what crows have pecked them here. He brags of his service as if he were of note: bring him to the king."

V-4

A British prison.

Two Jailers escort Posthumus into the cell and attach his ankle to a ring and chain.

The First Jailer says, "You won't be stolen now you have locks upon you; so graze as you find pasture."

The Second Jailer says, "Yes, or a stomach."

The Jailers leave laughing.

Posthumus says, "Most welcome, bondage; for you are a way, I think, to liberty: yet am I better than one that's sick of the gout; since he'd rather groan in perpetuity than be cured by that sure physician, death, who is the key to unbar these locks.

He grabs his head in both hands, "My conscience, you are shackled more than my ankles and wrists: You good gods, give me the means to pick that lock, then, I am free forever. Is it enough I am sorry? That's how fathers soothe their children; gods are full of mercy. Must I repent? I cannot do it better than in bonds, desired more than constrained: to satisfy, if of my freedom it is the main part, take no stricter accounting of me than my all. I know you are more merciful than vile men, who of their broken debtors take a third, a sixth, a tenth, letting them thrive again on their remainder: that's not my desire: for Imogen's dear life take mine; and though it is not as dear, it is a life; you created it: between man and man they weigh not every stamp; though light, take the coin for the sake of the image: you rather mine, being yours: and so, great powers, if you will take this audit, take this life, and cancel these cold bonds. Oh Imogen, I'll speak to you in silence."

He falls asleep.

110.

*

Apparitions appear:

The spirit of an old man, Sicilius Leonatus, dressed like a mighty soldier leads the spirit of Posthumus's mother by the hand to the head of the bed.

Two young men, also ghosts, Posthumus's brothers, approach the side of the bed. They are dressed for battle as they died.

Father looks to the heavens, "Show no more spite on mortal flies, you thunder-master, fall out with Mars, chide your wife, that your adulteries rates and revenges. Hasn't my poor boy, whose face I never saw, done nothing but good? I died while he obeyed nature's law and stayed in the womb. You should have been his father then–men say you are father to all orphans–and shielded him from this earthly suffering."

Mother cries out, "Goddess midwife Lucina didn't lend me her aid, but took me during my labour. Posthumus was ripped from me and came out crying amongst his foes, a thing of pity."

Father says, "Great nature, like his ancestry, moulded the stuff so well, that he deserved the praise of the world, as great Sicilius' heir."

The First Brother looks to the heavens, "Once he grew to manhood where in Britain was anyone that could be his parallel; or be a more promising object in the eye of Imogen, that could best judge his worth?"

Mother turns her eye to heaven, "For what reason was he mocked with marriage, to be exiled, and thrown from Leonati seat, and cast from his dearest, sweet Imogen?"

Father says, "Why did you allow Iachimo, slight thing of Italy, to taint his noble heart and brain with needless jealousy; and to become the contempt and scorn of the other's villainy?"

The Second Brother looks to the heavens, "We came from farther regions for this, our parents and the two of us, that fell bravely striking in our country's cause, our fealty and Tenantius' right to maintain with honour."

The First Brother says, "Like valorous service–brave deeds Posthumus has done for Cymbeline: then, Jupiter, you king of gods, why have you delayed the graces due for his merits, and turned them all to grief?"

Father says, "Open your heavenly window; look out; no longer exercise upon a valiant race your harsh and potent injuries."

Mother says, "Since, our son is good, Jupiter, take away his miseries."

Father says, "Peep out of your marble mansion; help; or we poor spirits will cry to the heavenly council against your deity."

The First Brother and The Second Brother say together, "Help, Jupiter; or we appeal, and fly from your justice."

An angry voice booms out from above. The living do not stir but the moaning spirits cower, "Offend our hearing no more, you petty spirits of the low region, hush!"

Jupiter descends in thunder and lightning, sat upon an eagle: he throws a thunderbolt. The apparitions fall on their knees.

Jupiter has a long face, high forehead, and prominent nose. A thin moustache flares from his nostrils over top of his mouth.

Jupiter says, "How dare you ghosts accuse the thunderer, whose bolt you know batters all rebellious coasts from the sky? Poor shadows, leave here, and rest upon your never-withering banks of flowers: don't

112.

be concerned about mortal events. It is no care of yours; you know it is ours. I cross whom I love best; to make my gift, the more delayed, delighted. Be satisfied that our godhead will uplift your low-laid son: his comforts thrive, his trials are over. Our star reigned at his birth, and he was married in our temple. Rise, and fade. He shall be lord of lady Imogen, and a great deal happier because of these afflictions."

In a flourish he "creates" a book with a gilded cover.

"Lay this tablet upon his breast, wherein his full fortune is foretold. So, I am away. No further noise about impatience, for fear you stir up mine. Mount, eagle, to my crystal palace."

And Jupiter is gone in a flash.

Father says, "He came in thunder; his celestial breath was sulphurous to smell: the holy eagle stooped as if to seize us in his talons: his ascension is more sweet than our blessed fields: his royal bird prunes the immortal wing and snaps his beak, as when his god is pleased."

The Apparitions all say, "Thanks, Jupiter," and vanish.

*

Posthumus wakes, "Sleep, you have been a grandsire, and begot a father to me; and created a mother and two brothers: but–oh mockery–gone, they went away as soon as they were born: and so I am awake.

"Poor wretches that depend on gods' favour, dream as I have done, wake and find nothing. But, sadly: many dream not to find, neither deserve, and yet are steeped in favours: so I am, that have this golden chance and don't know why. What demons haunt this ground?"

He discovers the book, "A book? Oh rare one, don't be, as is often in our gawdy world, a garment nobler than what it covers: let your effects so follow, to be, unlike our courtiers, as good as the promise."

He opens it and reads, "'When a lion's whelp shall, to himself unknown, without seeking find, and be embraced by a piece of tender air; and when from a stately cedar shall be lopped branches, which, being dead many years, shall after revive, be jointed to the old stock and freshly grow; then shall Posthumus end his miseries, Britain be fortunate and flourish in peace and plenty.'"

Posthumus says, "It is still a dream, or else the stuff madmen speak without thought; maybe both or nothing; or senseless speaking or a speaking such as sense cannot untie. Be what it is, the action of my life is like it, which I'll keep, if but for sympathy."

He puts the book in his pocket.

*

The First Jailer comes in, "Come, sir, are you ready for death?"

Posthumus says, "Rather over-roasted. I was ready long ago."

The First Jailer says, "Hanging is the word, sir: if you are ready for that, you are well cooked."

Posthumus says, "So, if I prove a good meal to the spectators, the dish pays the bill."

The First Jailer says, "A heavy reckoning for you, sir. But the comfort is, you won't be called for any more payments, fear no more tavern-bills; which are often the sadness of parting, as the procuring of mirth: you enter faint for want of meat, depart reeling with too much drink; sorry that you have paid too much, and sorry that you are too paid out; purse and brain both empty; the brain the heavier for being too light, the purse too light, being drawn dry of heaviness: you shall now be done with this contradiction. Oh, the charity of a penny rope, it sums up thousands in a trice: you have no true debtor and creditor but it; of what's past, is, and to come, the discharge: your neck, sir, is pen, book and coins; so the account is closed."

Posthumus says, "I am happier to die than you are to live."

The First Jailer says, "Indeed, sir, he that sleeps doesn't feel the toothache: but a man who was to sleep your sleep, and a hangman to help him, I think he would change places with his officer; because, you see, sir, you don't know which way you shall go."

Posthumus says, "Yes, indeed I do, fellow."

The First Jailer says, "Your death has eyes in his head then; I have not seen him pictured that way: you must either be directed by those that claim to know, or take upon yourself that which I'm sure you don't know, or risk the after inquiry on your own peril: and how your journey ends, I think you'll never return to tell."

Posthumus says, "I'll tell you, fellow, there are none want eyes to direct them the way I am going, they will wink and not use them."

The First Jailer says, "What an infinite joke this is, that a man should have the best use of eyes to see the way of blindness: I am sure hanging's the way of winking."

An Attendant appears, "Knock off his manacles; bring your prisoner to the king."

Posthumus says, "You bring good news; I am called to be made free."

The First Jailer jokes, "I'll be hanged then."

Posthumus says, "You shall then be freer than a jailer; no shackles for the dead."

The Attendant takes Posthumus out.

The First Jailer watches him leave, "Unless a man would marry a gallows and beget young gibbets, I never saw one so eager. Yet, on my conscience, there are worse scoundrels desire to live, even though he is a Roman: and there be some of them too that die against their wills; as would I, if I were one. I wish we were all of one mind, and one mind good; oh if only there were a lack of jailers and gallowses: I speak against my present profit, but my wish has progress in it."

V-5

Cymbeline's battle tent.

King Cymbeline enters with Belarius, Guiderius and Arviragus. The Lords, Officers, and Attendants with Pisanio follow.

Cymbeline says, "Stand by my side, you whom the gods have made preservers of my throne. Woe is my heart that the peasant soldier that fought so well, whose rags shamed those with gilded arms, whose naked breast stepped in front of shields of strength, can't be found: he'll be happy if we can find him, if our grace can make him so."

Belarius says, "I never saw such noble fury in so poor a thing; such precious deeds from one that promises nothing but beggary and sour looks."

Cymbeline says, "No word of him?"

Pisanio says, "He has been searched for among the dead and living, but no trace of him."

Cymbeline speaks to Belarius and the boys, "To my grief, I am the heir of his reward; which I will add to you, the liver, heart and brain of Britain, thanks to you she lives. It is now the time to ask where you are from."

Belarius says, "Sir, we are born of Cambria and gentlemen. To boast further would neither be true nor modest, unless I add, we are honest."

Cymbeline says, "Bow your knees."

The King passes his sword over their shoulders, "Arise knights of the battle: I make you companions to our person and will fit you with dignities becoming your estates."

Cymbeline sees Doctor Cornelius approaching with the Queen's Ladies and notes their severe nature, "There's business in these faces. Why do you greet our victory so sadly? You look like Romans, and not of the court of Britain."

Cornelius says, "Hail, great king, to sour your happiness, I must report the queen is dead."

The news, although expected, is still a jolt, "Who worse than a physician would this report favour? But I bear in mind medicine may prolong life, yet death will seize the doctor too. How did she die?"

Cornelius says, "With horror, madly dying, like her life, which, being cruel to the world, concluded most cruel to herself."

Cymbeline is upset by Cornelius's cold manner but Cornelius continues before Cymbeline can interrupt, "What she confessed I will report, so please you: these her women can correct me if I'm wrong; who with wet cheeks were present when she died."

He indicates the weeping Queen's Ladies.

Cymbeline calms, then cautiously, "Say."

Cornelius says, "First, she confessed she never loved you, only wanted the greatness got by you, not you. She married your royalty, was wife to your place; abhorred your person."

Cymbeline says, "She kept it to herself and had she said it while dying, I would not have believed it from her own lips. Proceed."

Cornelius says, "Your daughter, whom she pledged to love with such integrity, she confessed was a scorpion to her sight; whose life, except that her disappearance prevented it, she had planned to take by poison."

118.

Cymbeline says, "Oh most beautiful fiend! Who is it can read a woman? Is there more?"

Cornelius says, "More, sir, and worse. She confessed she had a deadly potion for you; which should feed on life by the minute and lingering, waste you by inches: during which she planned, by watching, weeping, tendering, kissing, to overcome you with her show, and when she had prepared you with her craft, to work her son into the adoption of the crown: but, by his strange absence she grew shameless-desperate; confessed her purposes to spite heaven and men; repented the evils she hatched that did not come about; so she died despairing."

Cymbeline says, "Ladies is that what you heard?"

The Queen's Lady says, "We did, so please your highness."

Cymbeline says, "My eyes were not at fault, for she was beautiful; my ears, that heard her flattery; nor my heart, which thought she was like she seemed; it would have been vicious to have mistrusted her: yet–oh my daughter–that it was my folly, you could say, and prove it in your feeling. Heaven mend all."

The captured Romans are brought forward under guard. Caius Lucius, Imogen, Iachimo, and the Soothsayer, along with the other prisoners, including Posthumus.

Cymbeline sets himself into his throne, "Caius, you haven't come now for the tribute that the Britons wiped out, though with the loss of many a bold one; whose families have asked that their good souls may be appeased with slaughter of you their captives, which ourself have granted: so think upon your estates."

Caius Lucius says, "Consider, sir, the fortunes of war: the day was yours by accident; had it gone with us, when the blood was cool, we wouldn't have threatened our prisoners with the sword. But since the gods will have it this way, that nothing but our lives may be called ransom, let it come: it suffices a Roman with a Roman's heart can suffer: Augustus lives to think on it: and so much for my personal care. This one thing only I will ask."

He pulls Imogen forward, "My boy, a born Briton, let him be ransomed: never has a master had a page so kind, so duteous, diligent, so tender over his occasions, true, so ready, so nurse-like: let his virtue join with my request, which, if I can be so bold, your highness cannot deny; he has done no Briton harm, though he served a Roman: save him, sir, and spare no other beside."

Cymbeline looks at Imogen, "I have surely seen him: he looks familiar. Boy, you have won my favour by your looks, and are my own. I don't know why, what reason, to say 'live, boy:' never thank your master; live: and ask of Cymbeline what blessings you wish, fitting your status, I'll give it; yes, even if you demanded a prisoner of the noblest taken."

He gestures toward Caius Lucius.

Imogen says, "I humbly thank your highness."

Caius Lucius says, "I do not ask you to beg for my life, good lad; and yet I know you will."

Imogen has spotted someone in the gathering and turns hard, "I'm afraid there's other work needs doing: I see something as bitter to me as death: your life, good master, must shuffle for itself."

Caius Lucius thinks, "The boy disdains me, he leaves me, scorns me: briefly die the joys of those that place them on the loyalty of boys and girls. Why does he stand so perplexed?"

Imogen is staring at Iachimo.

Cymbeline says, "What would you do, boy? I love you more and more: think more and more what's best to ask."

120.

He follows Imogen's gaze, "Do you know him? speak, will you have him live? Is he your family? your friend?"

Imogen says, "He is a Roman; no more family to me than I to your highness; who, being born your vassal, am something nearer."

Cymbeline says, "Why look at him so?"

Imogen says, "I'll tell you, sir, in private, if you please to give me hearing."

Cymbeline says, "Yes, with all my heart, and lend my best attention. What's your name?"

Imogen says, "Fidele, sir."

Cymbeline says, "Good youth, you are my page; I'll be your master: walk with me; speak freely."

Cymbeline and Imogen move aside to speak privately.

*

Belarius speaks to his sons, "Isn't this the boy revived from death?"

Arviragus says, "One grain of sand to another no more resembles that sweet rosy lad who died, and was Fidele."

He turns to his brother, "What do you think?"

Guiderius says, "The same that was dead is alive."

Belarius says, "Peace, peace, look closer; he doesn't look at us; creatures may look alike: if it were, I am sure he would have spoken to us."

Guiderius says, "But we saw him dead."

Belarius says, "Quiet; let's see what happens."

*

King Cymbeline and Imogen return and Pisanio recognizes her walk and mannerisms, "It is my mistress: since she is living, let the time run on to good or bad."

Cymbeline says, "Come, stand by our side; make your demand aloud."

He addresses Iachimo, "Sir, step forward; answer this boy, and do it freely; or, by our greatness, and the grace of it, which is our honour, bitter torture shall distinguish the truth from falsehood. On, speak to him."

Imogen says, "My wish is, that this gentleman tell who he had this ring from."

*

Posthumus, startled, wonders, "What's that to him?"

*

Iachimo is scared speechless.

Cymbeline says, "That diamond upon your finger, tell how you came by it?"

122.

Iachimo says, "You will torture me to leave unspoken that which, to be spoke, would torture you."

Cymbeline says, "Me? How?"

Iachimo says, "I am glad to be forced to say that which torments me to conceal. By villainy I got this ring: it was Leonatus' jewel; whom you banished: and which more may grieve you, as it does me: a nobler sir never lived. Will you hear more, my lord?"

Cymbeline says, "Everything that belongs to this."

Iachimo says, "That paragon, your daughter, for whom my heart bleeds, and my false spirits despair to remember. Give me leave; I faint."

Cymbeline says, "My daughter? what about her? Renew your strength: I'd rather you should live what nature allows than die before I hear more: strive, man, and speak."

Iachimo says, "Upon a time–it was an unhappy clock that struck the hour. It was in Rome–curse the mansion where we were. It was at a feast–oh, if only our meat had been poisoned–or at least those which I ate. The good Posthumus–what should I say? he was too good to be where bad men were; and was the best of all amongst those rare good ones–sitting sadly, hearing us praise our loves of Italy for beauty that made barren the swelled boast of him that could speak best. Features laming the shrine of Venus, or standing Minerva. Postures beyond nature, for character, a store of all the qualities that man loves woman for, besides that hook of wiving, beauty which strikes the eye–"

Cymbeline interrupts impatiently, "I stand on fire: come to the matter."

Iachimo says, "All too soon I shall, unless you would grieve quickly. This Posthumus, most like a noble lord in love and one that had a royal lover, took his hint; and–without dispraising those we praised, doing so he was as calm as virtue–he began his mistress' portrait; which by his tongue being made, and then a mind put in it, either our praised beauties were kitchen-trolls, or his description proved us to be unworthy sots."

Cymbeline says, "Get to the point."

Iachimo says, "Your daughter's chastity–there it begins–he spoke of her, as Diana had hot dreams, and she alone were cold: to which I, wretch, expressed doubt of his praise; and wagered pieces of gold against this," he indicates the ring, "which he wore upon his honoured finger, to attain the place of his bed and win the ring by hers and my adultery. He–true knight–no less confident of her honour than I truly found her–stakes this ring; and would so, even if it had been a carbuncle from Phoebus' wheel, and might safely do so, had it been as valuable as the whole chariot. Away to Britain I headed in this design: you may remember me at court; where I was taught by your chaste daughter the wide difference between amorous and villainous. Being quenched of desire, not hope, my Italian brain began to operate most vilely in your duller Britain; for my excellent advantage: and, to be brief, by trickery so prevailed, that I returned with enough proof to make the noble Leonatus go mad, by wounding his belief in her quality with tokens; describing notes of room-hangings, artwork, this her bracelet–oh cunning, how I got it–some secret marks on her body, so that he could not but think her bond of chastity quite broken, I took the prize. And then–"

A movement catches his eye, "I think I see him now–"

Posthumus advances on Iachimo in a rage, held by the guards, "Yes, so you do, Italian fiend. Ay me, most credible fool, reprehensible murderer, thief, any thing that's due to all villains past, present, and future. Oh, give me a rope, or a knife, or some poison, some thing to bring justice.

"You, king, send out for torturers ingenious: it is I that all the abhorred things of the earth improve by being worse than they. I am Posthumus, that killed your daughter: like a villain, I lie, that caused a lesser

124.

villain than myself, a sacrilegious thief, to do it. She was the temple of virtue; yes, and virtue herself. Spit, and throw stones, cast mire upon me, set the dogs of the street to bark at me: call every villain Posthumus Leonatus; and villainy as less than it was. Oh Imogen! My queen, my life, my wife. Oh Imogen, Imogen, Imogen."

Imogen runs toward him, "Peace, my lord; hear, hear–"

Posthumus sees the boy approach, "Shall we have a play of this? You scornful page, lie your part there."

He strikes her and she falls.

Pisanio rushes over to Imogen, "Oh, gentlemen, help me and your mistress: Oh, my lord Posthumus, you never killed Imogen until now. Help, help, my honoured lady."

Cymbeline says, "Is the world still going round?"

Pisanio uncovers Imogen's face to reveal her.

Posthumus says, "Why do I stagger?"

Pisanio says, "Wake, my mistress."

Cymbeline says, "If this is true, the gods mean to strike me to death with mortal joy."

Pisanio says, "How fare you mistress?"

Imogen sits up sharply when she sees Pisanio and pushes him, "Get away; you gave me poison: dangerous fellow, go, breathe not where princes are."

Cymbeline says, "Imogen's voice."

Pisanio says, "Lady, let the gods throw stones of sulphur on me, if that box I gave you was not the precious thing I thought it to be. The queen gave it to me."

Cymbeline says, "There's still more?"

Imogen says, "It poisoned me."

Cornelius cries out to Pisanio, "Oh gods! I left out one thing which the queen confessed. Which must prove you honest: she said: 'If Pisanio has given his mistress that potion which I gave him for medicine, she is served as I would serve a rat.'"

Cymbeline says, "What's this, Cornelius?"

Cornelius says, "The queen, sir, often asked me to make poisons for her, pretending the search for knowledge to kill only vile creatures of no esteem, like cats and dogs: dreading that her purpose was more dangerous, I made a compound for her, which, when taken, would cease the present power of life, but in a short time all natural offices would again do their due functions. Have you taken it?"

Imogen says, "Most likely I did, for I was dead."

*

Belarius says, "My boys, there was our error."

Guiderius says, "This is, sure, Fidele."

126.

*

Imogen approaches Posthumus, "Why did you throw your wedded lady from you?"

They embrace with all the passion of pent up desires.

Imogen says, "Imagine you are upon a rock; and now throw me again."

Posthumus holds her tighter and says, "Hang there like a fruit, my soul, until the tree dies."

Cymbeline says, "How now, my flesh, my child? What, do you make me a bystander in this? Will you not speak to me?"

Imogen runs to him, discarding her boy clothes and loosing her hair, she kneels, "Your blessing, sir."

*

Belarius speaks to Guiderius and Arviragus, "Though you did love this youth, I don't blame you: you had a reason for it."

*

Cymbeline says, "My tears fall as holy water on you; Imogen, your mother is dead."

Imogen says, "I am sorry for it, my lord."

Cymbeline says, "She was nothing; and it is because of her that we meet here so strangely: but her son is gone, we don't know how or where."

Pisanio steps forward, "My lord, now that fear has left me, I'll speak truth. When my lady went missing, Lord Cloten came to me with his sword drawn; foaming at the mouth, and swore my instant death if I did not reveal which way she went. By chance, I had a false letter of my master's; which led him to look for her on the mountains near Milford; where, in a frenzy, in my master's clothes, which he forced from me, he road away with sinful purpose and with an oath to violate my lady's honour: what became of him I don't know."

Guiderius steps forward despite Belarius's attempt to hold him.

Guiderius says, "Let me end the story: I killed him there."

Shocked, Cymbeline cries out in a whisper, "Jupiter, the gods protect. I don't want your good deeds paid from my lips by a harsh sentence: I ask you, valiant youth, deny it this time."

Guiderius says, "I have spoke it, and I did it."

Cymbeline's face falls, "He was a prince."

Guiderius says, "A most uncivil one: the wrongs he did me were not prince-like; he provoked me with words that would make me challenge the sea if it roared at me like that: I cut off his head; and am right glad he isn't standing here to tell his tale of my death."

Cymbeline says, "I am in sorrow for you: by your own tongue you are condemned, and must endure our law: you are dead."

128.

*

Imogen says, "I thought that headless man was Posthumus."

*

Cymbeline says, "Bind the offender, and take him from our presence."

Belarius steps forward boldly, "Stay, sir king: this man is better than the man he killed, his blood is as good as yours; and has more of your merits than a band of Clotens had ever taken scars for."

Belarius orders the guards, "Let his arms alone; they were not born for bondage."

The guards do not respond.

Cymbeline is upset, "Old soldier, why are you undoing the worth you haven't been rewarded for by tasting of our wrath? How can he be of blood as good as we?"

Arviragus says, "In that he spoke too far."

Cymbeline says, sadly, "And you shall die for it."

He gestures and the guards move in.

Suddenly the trio are in motion. They break free and stand back to back to back, ready to fight to the death barehanded.

Belarius says, "All three of us will die if I can't prove that two of us are as good as I have spoken of. My sons, I must, for my own part, unfold a dangerous speech, though it works out well for you."

Arviragus says, "Your danger is ours."

Guiderius says, "And our good his."

Belarius says, "Have at it then, by leave."

He addresses Cymbeline, "You had, great king, a subject who was called Belarius."

Cymbeline says, "What about him? He is a banished traitor."

Belarius says, "He has become this age. I agree he is a banished man. I don't know how he is a traitor."

Cymbeline looks closer and recognizes Belarius, "Take him away: the whole world shall not save him."

Belarius says, "Not too hasty: first pay me for the nursing of your sons; and let it be confiscated as soon as I receive it."

Cymbeline says, "Nursing of my sons?"

Belarius says, "I am too blunt and saucy." He kneels, "Here's my knee: before I rise, I will advance my sons; then you needn't spare the old man. Mighty sir, these two young gentlemen, that call me father and think they are my sons, are not mine; they are the issue of your loins, my liege, and blood of your begetting."

Cymbeline says, "How my issue?"

Belarius says, "As sure as you are your father's. I, old Morgan, am that Belarius you banished sometime ago: to do your pleasure was my only offence, my punishment itself, and all my treason; that I suffered was all the harm I did. These gentle princes–for such they are–these twenty years I have trained them: those arts they have as much as I could put into them; my breeding was, sir, as your highness knows. Their nurse, Euriphile, whom I wedded for the theft, stole these children when I was banished: I asked her to do it, having received the sentence in advance, for that which I did then: being beaten for loyalty incited me to treason: their deepfelt loss, the more of you it was felt, the more it suited my purpose of stealing them. But, gracious sir, here are your sons again; and I must lose two of the sweetest companions in the world. The blessings of these covering heavens fall on their heads like dew, for they are worthy to decorate heaven with stars."

Cymbeline says, "Your tears testify to your sincerity.

"The service that you three did is more worthy than the story you tell. I lost my children: if these are they, I don't know how I could wish a pair of worthier sons."

Belarius indicates Guiderius, "Be pleased awhile. This gentleman, whom I call Polydore, most worthy prince, is really Guiderius."

He indicates Arviragus, "This gentleman, my Cadwal, your younger princely son Arviragus; he, sir, was wrapped in a most curious shawl, made by the hand of his queen mother, which I can easily produce for more proof."

Cymbeline says, "Guiderius had a mole on his neck, a five pointed star; it was a mark of wonder."

Belarius pulls Guiderius over to show the mark on his neck to Cymbeline, "This is he; who still has that natural stamp upon him: it was wise nature's end in the donation, to be his evidence now."

Cymbeline turns to Imogen, "Oh, what, am I a mother to the birth of three? There was never a mother who rejoiced deliverance more. Blessed pray you be, that after this strange starting out of your orbits, may you reign in them now: Oh Imogen, you have lost a kingdom by this."

Imogen says, "No, my lord; I got two worlds by it."

Laughing, she rushes to Arviragus and Guiderius, "Oh my gentle brothers, have we been introduced? Oh, never say from now on except that in truth you called me brother when I was but your sister; I called you brothers when you were so indeed."

Cymbeline says, "Have you met before?"

Arviragus says, "Yes, my good lord."

Guiderius says, "And at first meeting loved; continued so, until we thought he died."

Cornelius says, "Because she swallowed the queen's potion."

Cymbeline says, "Oh rare instinct! When can I hear the whole story? This rapid summary has to it circumstantial branches, which should be rich in details. Where? and how did you live? And when did you go to serve our Roman captive? How did you part with your brothers? how did you first meet them? Why did you flee from the court? and where did you go?"

He turns to Belarius, "These, and the motives of you three in the battle, with I don't know how much more, should be demanded; and all the other by-dependencies, from chance to chance: but this is neither the time nor the place for our long discussions. See, Posthumus anchors upon Imogen, and she, like harmless lightning, throws her eye on him, her brother, me, her master; hitting each object with a joy: reflected several times over. Let's quit this ground, and smoke the temple with our sacrifices."

He goes to Belarius and puts his arm around him, "You are my brother and so we will hold you ever."

Imogen puts her arm around Belarius's other side, "You are my father too, and saved me, to see this gracious season."

Cymbeline says, "Everybody's happy except these in bonds: let them be joyful too, for they shall taste our comfort."

Imogen speaks to Caius, "My good master, I will yet do you service."

Caius Lucius says, "Happy be you."

Cymbeline says, "The peasant soldier, that fought so nobly, would have dignified this place, and honoured the gratitude of a king."

Posthumus takes out the sash and wraps it around his forehead and nose again, "I am, sir, the soldier that fought beside these three in meek worthiness; it was fitting for the purpose I then followed. That it was me, speak, Iachimo: I had you down and might have finished you."

Iachimo kneels before Posthumus, "I am down again: but this time my heavy conscience sinks my knee, as your force did then. Take that life, I beg you, which I so often owe: but your ring first; and here the bracelet of the truest princess that ever swore her faith."

He hands over the jewels.

Posthumus puts the ring on his finger and the bracelet on Imogen's arm.

Posthumus turns his attention back to Iachimo, "Don't kneel to me: the power I have over you is, to spare you; the malice towards you to forgive you: live, and deal with others better."

Cymbeline says, "Nobly doomed: We'll learn our freeness from a son-in-law; pardon is the word to all."

Arviragus addresses Posthumus, "You helped us, sir, as if you meant to be our brother; we are joyful that you are."

Posthumus says, "Your servant, princes."

Posthumus speaks to Caius Lucius, "Good my lord of Rome, call your soothsayer: while I slept I thought great Jupiter, astride his eagle, appeared with other spirits of my family."

He holds out the tablet, "When I woke, I found this on my chest; whose words are so hard to make sense of, that I can make no inference of it: let him show his skill in the deciphering."

Caius Lucius calls, "Philarmonus."

The Soothsayer appears from among the Roman prisoners, "Here, my good lord."

Caius Lucius says, "Read, and declare the meaning."

The Soothsayer reads aloud, "'When a lion's whelp shall, to himself unknown, without seeking find, and be embraced by a piece of tender air; and when from a stately cedar shall be lopped branches, which, being dead many years, shall after revive, be jointed to the old stock, and freshly grow; then shall Posthumus end his miseries, Britain be fortunate and flourish in peace and plenty.'"

He indicates Posthumus, "You, Leonatus, are the lion's whelp; the fit and apt deciphering of your name, being Leonatus, does mean so much."

He turns to Cymbeline, "The piece of tender air, your virtuous daughter, which we call 'mollis aer;' and 'mollis aer' we term it 'mulier:' which I translate as this most constant wife; who, even now, answering the letter of the oracle, unknown to you, unsought, were embraced with this most tender air."

Cymbeline says, "This has some meaning."

134.

The Soothsayer says, "The lofty cedar, royal Cymbeline, stands for you: and your lopped branches point at your two sons gone; who, stolen by Belarius, for many years thought dead, are now revived, joined to the majestic cedar, whose children promise Britain peace and plenty."

Cymbeline says, "We will begin with peace. And, Caius Lucius, although the victor, we submit to Caesar, and to the Roman empire; promising to pay our overdue tribute, which we were discouraged from by our wicked queen; whom the heavens, in justice, have laid a most heavy hand on both her and hers."

The Soothsayer says, "The fingers of the powers above do tune the harmony of this peace. The vision which I made known to Lucius, before the start of this yet scarce-cold battle, at this moment is fully accomplished; for the Roman eagle, soaring aloft from south to west, lessened herself, and vanished in the beams of the sun: which foreshadowed our princely eagle, the imperial Caesar, should again unite his favour with the radiant Cymbeline, which shines here in the west."

Cymbeline says, "Praise the gods; and let our crooked smokes climb to their nostrils from our blessed altars. We proclaim this peace to all our subjects. From now on: let a Roman and a British ensign fly friendly together: and march so through London-town: and in the temple of great Jupiter we will ratify our peace; seal it with feasts. March on there: Never was a war ended, before bloody hands were washed, with such a peace."

ABOUT THE EDITOR

J. Aldric Gaudet is an author, screenwriter and screenwriting lecturer.

His books include *Lug's Christmas Carol*, a peek at what Christmas ornaments get up to when left on their own; *Knighn* an imaginary adventure in a wonder land; and *Madmen Have No Ears: The Story of Shakespeare's Romeo and Juliet*.

His screenplay, *Anatomy of a Hijacking*, a political thriller about the most unusual, and most tragic, airplane hijacking pre-911, is stranded in DEVELOPMENT.

His initial screenplay for *Baltic Storm* starring Donald Sutherland, Greta Scacchi, and Jürgen Prochnow, was used to finance the production.

He wrote and directed two low budget movies, *Deadly Pursuit* and *The Hijacking of Studio Four*.

For TV he wrote the documentary series, *Struggle Beneath the Sea,* an episode of *The Littlest Hobo* and elements for the science series *What Will They Think of Next*.

He teaches *ScreenWriting123*, an intensive series of courses for storytellers of the screen. The course was developed from his McMaster University lecture series *Screenwriting Rules!*

For more information visit: http://www.jaldricgaudet.com